_he Ke,    ..ıng Jack_ is re...
ıacts... A brilliant read and an author to watch!'

Alison Brumwell, Chair of
CILIP Youth Libraries Group

'Jozefkowicz writes wonderfully about
family, friendship and self-discovery...'

*The Bookseller*, on *The Key to Finding Jack*

'Tackling food poverty and online bullying head on,
and featuring a puppy called Sausage (I can't even
speak for the genius of it all), I dare to defy anyone
who will not instantly fall in love with Erin
and her fellow detective buddies...'

Onjali Q. Raúf, BookTrust Writer in Residence,
on *The Cooking Club Detectives*

'Celebrating the importance of community, family
and friends, [*The Cooking Club Detectives*] is a
lovely, warm-hearted story that shows how
food can bring people together.'

*The Week Junior*, Book of the Week

'Sensitively tackling themes of online bullying
and food poverty, this is a heartfelt story about the
importance of community and the power of food to
connect people. With recipes dotted throughout...
[it] is also perfect for encouraging children
to get active in the kitchen.'

*Scotland on Sunday*

# The Dragon in the Bookshop

Ewa Jozefkowicz grew up in Ealing and studied English Literature at UCL. Her debut novel, *The Mystery of the Colour Thief*, was shortlisted for the Waterstones Children's Book Prize, 2019. Her second, third and fourth novels, *Girl 38: Finding a Friend*, *The Key to Finding Jack* and *The Cooking Club Detectives* are also published by Zephyr. Ewa lives in London with her husband and twin daughters and regularly visits family in Poland.

Also by Ewa Jozefkowicz

*The Mystery of the Colour Thief*
*Girl 38: Finding a Friend*
*The Key to Finding Jack*
*The Cooking Club Detectives*

# The Dragon in the Bookshop

## Ewa Jozefkowicz

ZEPHYR

*An imprint of* Head of Zeus

Head of Zeus Ltd
5–8 Hardwick Street
London EC1R 4RG

WWW.HEADOFZEUS.COM

*He was everywhere.*

*In the scratch of his claws as he turned in his sleep.*

*In the sparks from his nostrils that cut the night like lightning.*

*In the smoke, which hung in the air like a dark cloud, heralding doom.*

*But most of all, he was the fear of every inhabitant of the town, as they closed their shutters tight, barricaded their doors with sacks of flour, and burned incense, hoping that he would stay away.*

*He didn't, of course.*

# 1

I saw it on the small platform of rock near the lighthouse, in an area that could sometimes only be reached by boat because of the tides. I don't know what drew me to that pocket of darkness. I levered myself down, my fingers sliding clumsily over the slippery stone ledge. For a few horrible seconds I hung, suspended. I braced myself for the smack of icy sea water, but – miraculously – my left foot found a hold and I jumped across, landing exactly where I wanted to be.

Up close, I was certain of what it was. Three-pronged, like a bird claw, only much, much bigger. I put my hand inside the print. My fingers looked comically small in comparison. I traced the edge of it and felt a definite ridge. Excitement fizzed through me and something else too. On this outcrop of rock, time felt frozen and for a moment, I too had become timeless. I shut my eyes against the brisk Channel wind and felt as though my hand was taking root in the rock.

What animal had made the print and when? My instinct was to run home and ask the only person who might know. Dad would be even more ecstatic about the discovery. He'd take measurements, guide me on how to get the best photos and know *just* the book to consult for the answer.

Then I remembered. It was a punch in the chest. My happiness began to seep away, like water from a leaking bottle. These moments of forgetting were happening less, but when they did, they were as bad as the first time.

I took a few deep breaths. Whenever I was brought back to reality, I would stop what I was doing, go to my bedroom, lie on my bed and try not to think about anything for a while. If I was at school, I'd take myself to the loo to be alone. But my discovery today seemed so special, and I'd gone to so much effort to get here.

I hovered on the rock, looking at the print. Sea-salt spray flecked my cheeks and stung my eyes, but I felt proud to have found this place. Nobody knew about it except me. It was almost too good to be true. Eventually, I found my phone and took a photo of the print, then another, zooming in and out, amazed by how the light caught the edges of the central claw. That was when the second intriguing thing happened. I heard singing – a whistle on the wind in a language I didn't understand. The tune was unlike anything I'd ever heard. It was happy and sad, and I didn't want it to stop. Something pulled me towards the sound like a magnet.

I clambered back on to the ledge, emerging into the real world from a secret, mythical land, full of wonder and possibility. Had I really discovered a prehistoric print? Would it still be there next time I went to look for it?

I scanned the horizon to see where the singing might have come from. But the beach was empty and there was nothing except shingle stretching all the way to Ocean Drive. Even the fishermen who sometimes sat on the pier weren't here today.

The wind swooped through this barren landscape, like a looter swiping the spoils from a deserted battleground. It lifted a couple of empty tins and threw them against the bins of the lobster shack, causing a sudden rattle that startled me. Then it grabbed an old fishing net and danced with it around the upturned boat, before tiring and clearing itself a space to sleep among the reeds.

My breath escaped in white puffs. It would be Easter soon, even though it still felt like January. The singing soared again, carried by the crash of the waves and the cries of the seagulls. I was drawn to it and filled with an odd warmth.

As I listened, it seemed to be coming from further inland, near the old, upturned train carriage on the edge of the marshes, a remnant of the disused railway line that ran along the shore. I started running, which was stupid, of course – running through shingle is nearly impossible and I had to dig myself out with every step. The area we live in has been described by nature experts as England's version of the Sahara Desert, because of the sand and shingle stretching for miles to the sea. On a clear evening at sunset, the ground has a reddish tinge and I feel like I'm walking on the surface of Mars.

When I was younger, Dad and I used to pretend that it *was* Mars and that the nuclear power station in the distance was the first living unit, which the early settlers had made their home. It had titanium walls, water beds and robots who served meals. When the red-dust storms started, you had to hope that you would make it back to the unit. Sometimes I pretended a little too much and when the wind started up, I'd race home with my hands over my eyes. Then Dad would grab me round the waist and lift me over our front porch, shouting, 'We made it! The intrepid explorer is home!' That's what he always called me, and it was only when I was seven or eight that I admitted I didn't know what 'intrepid' meant. Dad explained that it is somebody who is bold and fearless, and I remembered being pleased. From then on, I always tried to be intrepid.

When I finally made it to the train carriage, the singing had stopped and there was nobody around. A chill went through me. It was weirdly quiet. Mum always walked carefully past the carriages. She believed they were haunted by the ghosts of drivers who'd met with misfortune on the railways. I knew they were just lumps of metal junk, which the boys in the year above liked to hang out in over the summer, but today I had a strong sense that there was someone else here. I checked the marshes and even walked round the empty shack that used to be an ice-cream shop. Nobody. Peering through the murky window, my heart hammered. Dust motes danced in the faint light coming in through the glass opposite. All I could see were rolled-up fishing nets and a couple of empty buckets. I decided to give up and go home.

My head was full of the print, as well as the singing, and I allowed my feet to think for me. I found myself walking in the direction of Ocean Drive, which used to be home, but wasn't any more. A new family had moved in, and someone else had my bedroom with its out-of-this-world sea view. If I shut my eyes, I could still see the waves lapping gently on the shore and hear Dad's voice behind me: 'If you squint you can just see France.'

My stomach clenched and I tried to brush the memory away, as I walked towards the small green deckhouse which is our new home. It's a poor substitute for 9 Ocean Drive. For a start, it only has one floor, is further inland and the small sliver of sea that can be glimpsed from the living room window is obstructed by other houses.

When Mum said that we had to sell up, I thought we might at least move somewhere new. Maybe to a town, or to Scotland, where Grandpa Dennis lives. Anything would have been better than staying here, where everything was supposed to be the same – school, the bookshop, the beach – only it wasn't, not any more. It was as if there were two universes separated by 4 November. The universe from 3 November was the real one, where I desperately wanted to be. And the universe from 5 November was a bad copy, because a key part was missing, and everything was distorted, like a painting left out in the rain. I could still see the outlines of people and things, but their edges had blurred and the sounds they made were muffled.

Mum insisted that we stayed. 'This is our place, Kon,' she'd said in a determined way, and nothing would change her mind.

She was already home when I arrived, which was weird because she didn't shut the bookshop until five-thirty p.m. When I came in she was sitting at the table, her phone to her ear, fingers nervously drumming the tabletop.

'There you are, Kon, thank goodness. Where have you been? I thought you'd come straight from school. You weren't picking up your phone so I rang Jomar and Ravi's parents to see if you'd gone to one of their houses. I was worried sick.'

She came over to hug me, but I didn't feel like hugging her, so she ended up awkwardly enveloping me.

I wanted to tell her about the print, but she wouldn't be interested. Somehow my excitement turned to anger. It was as if Mum didn't know anything about me any more. If she did, she would have remembered that I hadn't gone to Jomar or Ravi's houses since before … well, since 3 November.

In this new blurry universe, Mum and I were like a couple of planets whose inhabitants were too far away to hear one another and had given up sending satellite signals.

'Don't do it again, Kon. Please. I have to be able to rely on you. There's too much—'

She broke off and went over to the cupboard, pretending to get things ready for tea. She fumbled around and I knew it was so I didn't see her crying. I should have gone and given her a hug, but I didn't.

'Sorry,' she said, finally turning around. 'I'm just finding the bookshop a bit much. The figures aren't adding up again. I need to hire an accountant. It will cost extra money, of course, which we don't have.'

She breathed in. 'I'm seriously thinking that we should sell A Likely Story.'

*No!* My head spun with what this might mean. Another house move, an even smaller place? I'd wanted to move away at first, I know, but not now. Not far from the rocks and shingle and all of Dad and my discoveries.

'It's never been my thing, Kon. I wanted to make it work – we both want it to work…'

She tried to grasp my hand, but I snatched it away.

'What do I know about books? Or even how to run a shop? I've never done it in my life, and I'm not made for it, as it turns out. There are fewer and fewer customers. It was always your dad who drew people in... It isn't what it used to be, Kon. And it makes me sad and anxious to see how empty it is. I don't want us to go bankrupt.'

There were so many hot, angry words spilling from my brain to the tip of my tongue. But as always the barricades came down.

I stopped speaking the day after Dad died. I never planned for it. It just happened. When I first found out he was gone, I screamed and screamed. Mum tried to hold me tight, but I pushed her away and shut the door to my room. Later, when she asked whether I wanted to go to hospital to see him one final time, I tried to say, 'No,' but I couldn't get the word out. It was almost as though, if I didn't say anything, maybe it wouldn't be true. Because the last thing I wanted was to admit that it *was*. I didn't speak the next day, or the one after that. I stayed silent through the funeral, as everyone patted me on the back and said how sorry they were. I refused to do a reading. Mum went back to work, and I went back to school and all the while I remained drifting quietly through my dark universe. The silence was my cocoon: it was comforting, and I could control it.

In those first weeks, I could tell that Mum was certain my voice would come back. When we emerged from the horrible chaos of moving house and sorting out A Likely Story, she sat me down and said that she missed talking to me. I wanted to tell her that I missed talking to her too. She asked if I wanted to speak to someone different. Maybe a counsellor? I shook my head. Didn't she understand? I didn't want to speak *at all*. She left my room looking worried and shaken. So later I slipped a note under her door saying: *Give me some time.*

It's been months since that happened, and she hasn't asked me again. She adapted by communicating with me in a different way, like Jomar and Ravi, which involved a lot more talking on their part. Not speaking was my only possible language. It worked for me, except for when I was really, really mad. Like now, when the words boil up inside and I feel I am bursting with them.

'Stephen's been doing his best to support me,' Mum continued, 'but he and his wife want to move north before the baby comes. He's been honest about that. I thought that instead of hiring someone new, it would make sense to find a good buyer for the shop.'

I stared at the table. My eye was caught by a knot in the wood that looked like a mountain cave, and I forced myself to concentrate on it, instead of looking at Mum. Because if I did, something inside me would crack and I would split down the middle.

*Don't sell. Don't sell. Don't sell*, ran on a loop through my mind. If Mum cared about Dad at all she would want to keep his bookshop. She would make it work somehow. Run more events, do better window displays.

'I wish you would talk to me,' said Mum in a tired voice. 'How am I supposed to know what you're thinking? If I have to go around guessing, then my guess is that it's OK to mention the bookshop sale to you as an idea, because you haven't been there for months. I thought maybe you wouldn't mind me letting it go.'

And that was when the words trapped inside me reached boiling point. I couldn't listen to Mum any longer; I couldn't even look at her. I turned and ran to my room.

2

As soon as I shut my bedroom door, regret flooded through me, and I started conjuring all the things I should have said. Because Mum *was* trying. She'd tried harder than most people would have to keep the bookshop going, only she didn't know how. Or maybe she couldn't muster the energy any more, just like I couldn't muster the words. But there had to be a way. If she was about to give up, what hope did either of us have?

And there was an important thing about A Likely Story which I knew she remembered. It was the last place in which Dad had been alive. It was a day that I replayed over and over in my mind until I couldn't stand it. It went like this.

Dad had been feeling a bit breathless at breakfast after getting back from his morning run. He'd joked that he was getting old, although he was younger than nearly all my friends' dads. When he'd walked me to school, I'd watched him out of the corner of my eye, because I could tell that something wasn't quite right. I saw the familiar crease in his forehead which appeared whenever he was worried. He'd asked if we could stop for a moment, and he'd sat on Mr Higgins' garden wall at the end of Ocean Drive.

'I just need a minute, Kon,' he'd said. 'I think I've got a touch of heartburn. I must have eaten too quickly after my run.' He was clutching his chest.

'I'll take you back home,' I'd told him, but he'd waved away the idea.

'I'll be fine, honestly. Plus, we have a new delivery of books today. I don't want to miss it. There are some awesome new titles that I want to tell you about.'

And for the rest of our journey to school, we talked about the new books that he was most excited to read. We'd played our usual game, 'Digging for Books'. He would describe his top three picks in three words and, based on his description, I would choose the order in which we'd read them. He would only reveal the titles at the end. I'd tried to focus on the game, but I couldn't, because the worried crease on his forehead hadn't disappeared.

'So long, Kon!' he'd said, giving me a smile at the gate and a high-five.

'Dad, will you come to the Guy Fawkes assembly?' I'd suddenly remembered. Dad had given me a book about the Gunpowder Plot a few weeks ago, which meant I had some extra facts up my sleeve that many of my classmates didn't. Such as Guy Fawkes wasn't the ringleader in the plot to blow up the House of Lords. It was actually a man called Robert Catesby.

'I wouldn't miss it for the Milky Way,' he'd replied, and I'd laughed, because he always tried to go one bigger than anything everyone else said.

'Are you sure you're going to be all right?' I'd asked him.

'Of course,' he'd said, hugging me tight.

'You're not just saying it?'

'I wouldn't *just* say anything to my best person without meaning it, would I?' he'd whispered into my hair, pulling me close, and I'd been reassured.

Because Dad never lied to me about anything, ever. He'd told me once that honesty and trust are vital, not only to being a great explorer, but for almost every element of life. So I'd gone into school not even worrying much.

It had happened about two hours later, as he'd been serving a customer. His heart stopped and that was when my universe split into two. Stephen had reacted as quickly as he could, but it had been too late.

Thinking about Dad's final moments hardened the painful plug in my throat. I wondered what he'd thought. Was he scared? Did he want Mum and me next to him? On some days I managed to reassure myself that it had happened so quickly that he didn't feel it, but today wasn't one of them. The thought of Dad in the bookshop, keeling over in pain, made me feel physically sick.

As this awful image surfaced in my mind, the sound of the doorbell ringing splintered it. I could hear that it was Millie, Mum's friend from the hair salon where she used to work. She came to 'check in' on us a few times a week, which I hated because she always asked me lots of questions, though, of course, I never answered. It didn't stop her asking. I put my headphones on to drown out their talking and grabbed my phone to look at the claw print. I imagined how my conversation with Dad would have gone.

'Check it out, Dad. I knew it was a fossil!'

'Kon – that is *huge*, but also completely invisible unless you're practically looking straight at it. How did you spot that?'

'The sun was reflecting off the surface of the rock and I could just about see one of the claw marks. What do you reckon it is?'

'Come on, tell me the facts that you've managed to gather. Let's go through them.'

I liked this about Dad. He had a scientific mind. He liked to collect all the information and put it in order.

'It's a three-pronged print. The claws are curled. It's about five times as big as my hand. I spotted it on the rock ledge near the water.'

'Hmmm. It looks too big to belong to a Baryonyx, and the wrong shape for a Dacentrurus.

I guess it could be a Megalosaurus. If only we had the professor with us...'

The professor was what Dad called Professor Jim Jacobsen, the most famous UK dinosaur expert.

'Yeah, but we have the next best thing – his books.'

'Exactly. D'you want to go to the bookshop and have a look?'

'Sure.'

And suddenly I had such a longing to hear Dad's voice for real and not just in my head that I did something I hadn't done before. I switched on his old tablet and found the audio files of bedtime stories he'd recorded for me when I was much younger. Before Dad owned the bookshop, he'd worked for a publisher and often had to travel. Mum always read to me before bed, and she was great at doing the funny poems, but Dad was best at the longer stories and the voices of the different characters. So he'd recorded himself reading some of my favourite books for the times he was away from home.

I saw them now as file names on the screen. I pressed Play.

# 3

'I have a new football kit,' said Jomar, as we walked into town. He still came to get me on the way to school every morning, even though I never replied as he chatted. I wanted to, but the words that were on the tip of my tongue somehow sounded wrong. And the longer I was silent, the more impossible it seemed for me to speak.

Jomar has been my friend since we were five and we've always done everything together. In the old days, neither of us would shut up on the walk to school. Sometimes we would be laughing or talking so loudly that Mrs Henderson, the old lady who lived at the end of School Way, would tut at us. But recently it felt as if everything we'd talked about was silly and unimportant. I was scared that if I opened my mouth, Jomar would realise this and be upset. I so didn't want him to be upset.

'Yeah,' he continued, as though I'd asked a question. 'My uncle is over from the States and gave it to me. It's Messi, obviously. I was thinking of asking for Kane, but in the end, I thought, Messi is my man. Hey, shall I ask if he can get you a Lewandowski kit?'

Lewandowski is my top player, and he was Dad's too. They came from the same hometown. I used to be a pretty good striker, but my heart wasn't in the game any more and I kept missing passes.

I shook my head.

Jomar shrugged and carried on regardless, talking about what he and his uncle would be doing that weekend. This was what our school journeys had been like over the past few months. Jomar talked, and I listened. Or sometimes, when he'd run out of things to say, we walked in silence. He didn't seem to mind.

Today, the first lesson was maths with Mr Karamo, which I like, mainly because there are right and wrong answers for everything. We'd started learning trigonometry and I could get my head down and work on figuring out the missing angle. It took my mind off things.

The only downside was that Luke was sitting in front of me and he'd been acting strangely towards me for a while. Maybe he thought *I* was acting strangely by not speaking. But he was getting worse. He didn't make nasty jibes behind my back now; he waited until he knew I'd hear them.

Luke lived next door to our old house in Ocean Drive and we used to hang out all the time, even though Jomar and Ravi were never that keen on him. We'd go kite surfing on the beach and spend hours on the massive trampoline in his garden. Luke had been in a different class to us, so we didn't see that much of each other at school. But I'd overheard Hannah, his mum, telling Dad that Luke had struggled to make friends and wasn't getting on with Mrs Zanetti, his teacher. That's probably why she'd asked to move him into our class after Christmas.

Maybe Luke had expected that I would look out for him now that we were in the same class. Maybe the old Konrad would have done. But I wasn't the old Konrad. Most days I could barely look out for myself. I don't think Luke understood that it was nothing to do with him, and he didn't take it well. I wanted to explain, but that would mean starting a conversation, which was something I couldn't do.

I was relieved when he made friends with Noah whose dad is our local GP. Luke had spent all of last month trying to impress him. But it hadn't stopped him from bothering me.

'Right,' said Mr Karamo. 'I have a challenge for those of you who might have already worked through the equations I've set. This requires a bit of extra consideration. But whoever cracks it the fastest will win a prize.'

That's why I like Mr Karamo. He's matter of fact and he gets on with things. On either side of me, Jomar and Ravi didn't even bother looking up at the whiteboard, but I noted down the equation and got to work.

The drawing had many missing angles, and the trick was to figure out how to get clues about them in order. I had to use the little information I had to work out the first angle and use that to get the next one, then the one after and so on. There was a method, but I had to make sure that I didn't get anything wrong on the way.

Luke is amazing at maths, and I could see him scribbling away furiously. I was curious about who would get the answer first. I worked through each step, one by one, but I still wasn't sure when I put my hand up.

I handed my sheet to Mr Karamo and I could see that he was impressed.

'Nice work, Konrad. Methodical and fast. You win a special trigonometry calculator.' He handed me the purple calculator and I felt a burst of pride.

'Good job,' said Ravi. 'I couldn't do any of it.'

Luke glared at me. 'I'll get you next time,' he muttered. 'Watch me.'

At break we split into teams for football and I joined in, even though I didn't feel like it. But I was late getting to the pitch with Jomar and Ravi, and the captains had already been decided – Luke, and Marcus, who was by far the best at football in our year and probably the entire school. They had four players each. Marcus picked Ravi. Luke picked Jomar, and I was left out.

'You can have an extra player,' said Marcus to Luke. 'I don't mind. It's only a quick kick around.'

'I don't want Mowgli on my team,' said Luke.

'I'm sorry, what?' asked Jomar.

'You know – Mowgli, the wild boy,' he said, grinning and glancing over at me. 'He's abandoned civilisation to live on the beach in a fisherman's shack. He's gone so wild he doesn't even speak any more. I'd be surprised if he remembers how to play football.'

A deep red clouded my vision. I could still hear voices – Jomar's and Ravi's, coming in and out of focus like an old, faulty radio. They were shouting something at Luke, about what a horrible idiot he was being. Jomar said that he wasn't playing for his team, but I was no longer listening. I turned and ran back to the main school building, up to the loos on the top floor, where I locked myself in a cubicle for the rest of break, staring at the photo of the footprint on my phone. It calmed me down. Ravi found me before the bell went and put his arm round my shoulder.

'Ignore Luke. He isn't worth anyone's time,' he said. 'He's showing off to Noah. It's the most pathetic thing I've seen.'

I nodded.

But there was a new feeling in my stomach – fear. Sitting in the cubicle, I'd realised that no matter how much time had passed since 4 November, things weren't any better. I'd thought that by now I might feel normal and want to start talking again, but I didn't. An idea began to dawn on me, working its way deeper and deeper into my frazzled mind – what if I *never* felt better? What if this new distorted universe would always be my world?

After break, we had geography where we were learning about geological formations. I listened, hoping that Mrs McInally might discuss the fossilised remains of animals and plants that were visible in some of these rocks, maybe even footprints. Instead, she showed us maps of the scary levels of erosion in different coastal areas.

'Careful the sea doesn't swallow you, Wild Boy,' whispered Luke, loudly enough for me to hear. I almost turned around and told him to shut up, but Jomar grabbed my shoulder.

'He's not worth it,' he repeated.

Then we had English and we were doing creative writing with Mrs Layton, who was telling us about structuring stories. She talked about how to create tension at the beginning, to draw your reader in. She went through the different challenges that you might set for your main character and how you should have a clear structure to your story, including a beginning, middle and end.

The old Konrad would have put his hand up and said that there's something else just as important as structure and shape. It's that every story comes from deep inside the writer – like a spark of their mind igniting the page. That's what Dad had told me on A Likely Story's opening day, when we'd sat together after the launch party – me, him and Mum, surrounded by books.

'Think how special it is to share this space with so many people,' he said, pointing at the shelves. 'You know, Kon, I believe that for every reader there is a character in a book somewhere that matches them almost exactly. It's just a case of finding them.'

I remember gazing around the bookshop in wonder, imagining all the possible worlds I could enter, the places I could travel to, the characters I could meet. I told Dad then how I thought stories were like magical gateways, which could take us anywhere we chose.

I could have said all of this to Mrs Layton, but instead I kept my mouth shut and got on with my work.

# 4

After school, Jomar and Ravi went to football club, but as I hadn't signed up, I went home by myself. I was glad to have the excuse to be alone.

I couldn't wait to see the claw print again. Maybe there were more. I hadn't even thought of thoroughly searching the surrounding area yesterday. For the first time that day, hope flared. I was the intrepid explorer, making a brilliant new discovery. Thoughts of Luke and school shrank from view.

The headland seemed peaceful, but I wasn't fooled. The growling wind beast was only napping. When it woke, it would probably blow stronger than ever, so I adjusted the collar of my coat, just in case. I took the bus which dropped me off by the café, where Dad used to buy us crab sandwiches on Saturdays when Mum was working. There were two fishermen sitting on the benches outside. As they spoke, cloudy huffs of air formed around them.

The smell here made my stomach rumble every time. It was a delicious mix of saltwater and sweet, toasted brioche buns. I imagined that heavenly first bite. It looked like the seagulls were thinking the exact same thing, as they swept down towards the fishermen with a hungry *huoh-huoh-huoh*.

I marched through the shingle to the rock ledge. Without the wind, it was a lot easier than the last time. I wedged my rucksack beneath a reddish speckled stone that jutted towards the lighthouse like a mini pier. It would be safe there from the wind and waves.

I was about to lower myself down from the ledge when I heard it, the singing, louder this time, and clearer. The tune was the same, but it sounded somehow sadder than before. I needed to find out where it came from. Instinctively, I turned in the direction of the two ponds, which Mum calls the Eyes of the Sea.

That was when I saw her, a girl, kneeling beside the pond. And as she peered intently into the water, she sang – a delicate and unearthly sound, it seemed the most natural thing in the world. Was I imagining her? But since she didn't disappear, I supposed she must be real. She had light brown skin and long, flowing, curly black hair. She was wearing a brightly patterned dress and no coat, and looked so completely out of place on the freezing marsh that I almost laughed.

Sometimes the odd birdwatcher could be seen around here, but it was mostly deserted, especially on cold days like today. This girl was completely ignoring the weather and seemed so absorbed in her own world that she hadn't noticed me coming. Good. The last thing I wanted was another person who expected me to speak to them. I should have backed away, but I was fascinated and drew closer.

She had a magnifying glass and a large jar. Something black and slimy was wriggling inside it. She'd stopped singing and now seemed to be talking to it.

'*Olá, amigo. Eu apenas quero ver você.*'

I was about to back away when my foot caught a clump of marsh grass and I landed with a crunch, bottom first.

The girl turned and looked straight at me. I felt my face burning. She smiled, not the usual sort of smile when you meet a stranger. She smiled as if she was genuinely happy to see me. I noticed the freckles on her nose and that her front tooth was chipped.

'Do you want to see him?' she asked. 'I was telling him not to be scared. I'm only taking a look, then I'll release him.'

I leaned in and realised what was in the jar. A leech. A shudder went through me, which she noticed, because she laughed.

'Ah, you don't like him because he's slippery. But this is a special guy. He's a medicinal leech,' she said. 'You know, it's the only leech in this country that can suck blood from humans. In my avó's – that's my grandmother's – day, they used to believe that leeches could extract bad blood from people and leave only the good behind. This is one of the few places left in Europe where you can still find them. Isn't that fantastic?'

She seemed so excited to be sharing her leech with me. I tilted my head and couldn't help smiling enthusiastically. But I didn't say anything. Luke darted into my mind. If what she was saying was true, he could definitely do with some leech treatment.

The girl released the leech gently into the water.

'Look among those grasses. Can you see a flash of blue?' she asked. I couldn't until she pointed it out. '*Anax imperator*. Isn't it a wonderful name? That's Latin. In English it's called the emperor dragonfly. You can barely see its wings because they beat thirty times per second. Incredible, don't you think?'

When I still didn't reply, she looked at me, as if to check that I was listening, and smiled again.

'Do you live near here?' she asked.

I nodded.

'Ah, you are lucky. I'm new. We arrived three weeks ago. I was scared at first about what it would be like. I really didn't expect this,' she said, gesturing around her. 'It doesn't feel like England. My dad said that we were going to live in the English desert. I thought he was joking. He is a conservationist of endangered species and I thought: what could there be to conserve in a desert?' She laughed again. It was a nice laugh – melodic, like the song I'd heard her sing.

'But it wasn't a joke,' she continued. 'These tiny stones everywhere, made by sea waves working their way over the land for thousands of years. You would think that nothing should survive here and yet so much does. Why?'

I considered her question. I liked how she spoke so precisely, as if every word mattered. I wanted to answer her, but the truth was that I had no idea what she meant. The way she was talking, it was as if there was a jungle all around us, when it was just shingle, with a bit of water and dried grass thrown in. Maybe that was the clue?

She didn't wait for me to answer.

'There are so many species that are invisible to most people. Which means that they are well hidden from predators. But you're lucky, because I know how to look for them. Come with me.'

I followed her round the edge of the pond to where the reeds grew highest. We sat cross-legged, our knees nearly touching. Neither of us spoke.

The wind whipped over our heads. I was suddenly aware of the sounds of the marshes, so full of life, and the waves crashing in the distance.

She pointed between two blades of grass and whispered, 'A short-haired bumble bee. I spotted one earlier today. They're excellent pollinators. I wonder how many plants on the marshes exist thanks to this guy? Hundreds, I imagine. Maybe more. And they'll go on to create their own pollen, and the whole cycle of life will start again. You know, everything in nature leaves a little bit of itself behind. It rubs off – quite literally – on the world around it, which means that it's never really gone.'

Like books, I thought to myself. Dad used to say that in books, authors leave pieces of themselves behind for others to find. As I listened to the girl, I felt as if I was seeing the world around me for the first time. There was so much to learn and explore in this place that I thought I knew it like the back of my hand.

She got up and brushed down her skirt. Her bare knees between where her dress ended and her wellingtons began were covered in bruises and dirt.

'It was nice to meet you,' she said, holding out her hand. I felt myself smiling. 'Meet me here tomorrow? I have something else I want to show you.'

I nodded without thinking and as she turned to walk in the direction of the old crab café, I wanted to run after her and ask her a million questions. Who was she? Where was she from? Why didn't she wear a coat? What was she singing? And in what language? Would she definitely come back?

The questions were bubbling in my mind, brimming in my throat.

She turned around.

'By the way, my name's Maya,' she said. 'See you tomorrow.'

I watched as a slight wind caught her dark, tight curls and threw them in her face. She skipped over the shingle in her ridiculously oversized wellingtons as if it was no effort. By the time she was level with the lighthouse, she was singing again.

5

When I got home, Mum told me off for being late again.

'Was it maths club?' she asked, trying to contain her irritation and give me the benefit of the doubt. 'I forget what days you do these things.'

I nodded and immediately felt awful for lying. In my head, I apologised to Dad.

'Show me your timetable and I can pick you up if you'd like. We should make the most of me closing the bookshop early this week. Maybe we could go to dinner at Alf's one of these days? We haven't been there for ages. You could tell me about what you've been up to at school. We could catch up properly.'

Alf's is the best fish and chip shop around. They do crab rolls to die for and incredible triple-cooked chips. The last time we'd been there, Dad had ordered us the catch of the day which was the most enormous cod I'd seen. Even the three of us couldn't manage it. I didn't know why Mum wanted to go there to 'catch up'. It wasn't as if being in a different place would mean I'd suddenly talk.

I dug my homework diary out of my rucksack and showed her the timetable. Maths club today and Friday was tech club. I didn't intend to go to that either, but she didn't need to know that.

'OK, so maybe Saturday?' she asked hopefully.

I nodded. Maybe I'd think of an excuse before then. I felt a flash of guilt. Mum was only trying to spend time with me. But I knew what she'd want to talk about. And I couldn't say a word about that.

'Kon,' said Mum. I saw her picking at the skin around her fingernails which was a sign that she was nervous.

'Kon, I'm sorry that you feel so strongly about the bookshop,' she said. 'I didn't realise that it meant such a lot to you. Because, you know, you've never mentioned it…'

She'd come into my room late last night after I'd stormed out. She'd cooked an omelette and brought it up as a late-night treat, because she was worried I'd skipped dinner.

I'd faced the wall and pretended to be asleep.

'You're probably wondering why I don't try harder,' she continued. 'I've never run a shop before. It should be easy, but it isn't. I could learn, of course. I could ask Stephen to teach me the accounts and how to manage the stock. But I don't know anything like what your dad used to know about books. He was so good with the customers. They called him the matchmaker, didn't they? Because he could always match a person with a book he knew they'd love.'

I smiled at the memory. It was Luke's older sister, Sally, who'd first called Dad that. He recommended so many books to her that she barely had time to surface for air. Dad loved the nickname and he'd even put a sign in the window which said: *Come in and chat to the one and only book matchmaker.*

Sometimes when the little kids came in all excited, he put on a special cloak he'd made from an old curtain and took out a crystal ball with a book inside it, which he'd picked up at some antique fair. He was a book wizard, for sure.

Mum was right that she couldn't do that. I couldn't either. I'm not sure anyone could, except Dad.

All of a sudden I longed to see the bookshop again – to stand in that cosy space one last time, breathing in the warm, woody smell.

I decided to go on Saturday afternoon, before Stephen closed for the day.

Next day I refused a lift home from Jomar's mum. She and Jomar would wait to see me safely into my house when they dropped me off after school, and there was no way that Mum would let me out on the marshes again. Now that she'd taken to closing the bookshop early, she was always there when I got home.

I'd looked forward to seeing Maya all day. She was so different from everyone I'd ever known.

I decided she didn't belong to my dark universe from 5 November. She didn't belong to the one before 4 November either. She seemed to be from somewhere else entirely, and that was a comforting thought. Perhaps I could ask her to come with me to A Likely Story. I wondered what she would think of it. I hadn't been there for five months, two weeks and six days. Would it still look and smell the same?

I was worrying about this when I got to the marshes and realised that Maya was nowhere to be seen.

My eyes darted around the lake, looking for a bright dress among the reeds, but there was nothing. The orange-grey of the shingle mixed with the green spikes of the marsh grass, and the wind howled as it ran through the deserted, rusting train carriage. Disappointment settled in the pit of my stomach.

I should have known. Why would somebody as awesome as Maya be interested in someone like me? She'd probably already forgotten about our meeting.

I walked around the train to make sure she wasn't there. I felt mad at myself for feeling so hopeful. An old pink fishing net was hanging despondently from the carriage roof. Around the left-hand side, a dirty hoodie had been left behind, half-hidden in the shingle. There was a huge, graffitied beer keg, some crushed tins, what looked like a broken African drum, and a full-length mirror, with a horizontal crack running down the middle, propped against the wall. My reflection looked back at me, white and searching.

'Don't be stupid. Go home,' I muttered. I remembered my promise to Mum, which I was already breaking. I knew that soon I wouldn't have an excuse to come here. It was my last chance to check whether there were any other prints.

Stuffing my fists deep inside my pockets and with my face lowered against the elements, I walked against the wind in the direction of the rock ledge. Climbing down was far easier this time. My feet seemed to know where to step.

The footprint was still there and, if anything, seemed clearer and more defined. I traced its glistening edge with my finger. Surely, there had to be more. I climbed down on to the second rock ledge so that I was almost level with the sea, but, straight away, it was obvious it wasn't a good idea.

I could hear Dad's voice: 'No point looking there. The sea might have washed them away, Kon. Come on, intrepid explorer, think harder about where they could be.'

I was about to climb up when I glanced at the sea. The grey-blue rolling waves were swelling. A lonely seagull hovered above the water, the freezing wind propelling it towards the shore.

Something urged me to get in. It was a stupid thing to do in this weather, but the tide was low, so I decided to take the risk. I left my shoes and socks next to the print and stood at the water's edge, waiting for the rush of waves over my feet, and the slimy pull of seaweed tugging at my toes. It was so sudden and so cold that I cried out. Without thinking, I took two steps in, then another two. The stony surface gave way to shingle. Each wave swirled around my ankles in little eddies and sucked at my feet before drawing back into the sea.

Suddenly, in a burst of memory so powerful that I could feel him there next to me, Dad said, 'You, me and the sea.' He breathed in, pretending that we were having a moment of quiet, then grinned as he shouted, 'Race you to the crab café!'

'Hey!'

For a split-second, I thought it was Mum's voice from my daydream, calling us to the shore.

But then I saw Maya's head appear on the bank above the fossil stone. The wind hurtled in from the sea and her hair fanned her face like a lion's mane. She was pulling off her red wellingtons and climbing down to meet me.

'I'm sorry I'm late,' she shouted. 'I always forget to put my watch on. And I couldn't remember what time we met yesterday, so I didn't know when to come. I had to go by the sun.'

'You have to check where your shadow is,' she went on, almost as if she knew I wasn't going to answer. 'But it's not very exact, especially when it's cloudy. I see you decided to go swimming while you waited.' She stepped into the water next to me. She didn't even wince.

'Why don't you go swimming by the lighthouse? It's easier to get in over there. D'you know that the first day we arrived, I went out right to the end of the pier? There are little sand hills, so one minute the water is up to your waist and the next it only reaches your ankles.'

I wasn't here to swim, of course, and I hadn't been planning on showing the footprint to anyone, but Maya was different. Something told me that she could be trusted.

I beckoned her to come closer to the rock ledge and pointed.

She stood there, motionless, as if not daring to breathe.

'Whoa,' she said, staring at the print. Then, in a smooth movement, she lowered herself to the ground and jumped skilfully on to the ledge next to me. She ran her fingers over the print in the same way that I had, feeling for a ridge. The clouds suddenly parted and in the burst of sunlight that followed, the rock seemed to sparkle, as if the print had only recently been made.

'Look at the size of it. It's as if it belongs to a

dragon, if they existed. But it might have been made by a dinosaur.'

I could have hugged her. She was reading my thoughts. I nodded eagerly.

'Think how magical that would be,' she whispered. 'You need to get a specialist to look at it.' Her eyes lit up as if she'd remembered something important. 'Can I introduce you to someone?' she said.

I nodded again.

'Come up here.'

We put our shoes and boots back on to protect us against the shingle. As we climbed up the ledge and made our way towards the marshes, I wondered whether she was going to take me to meet her dad. Maybe he knew something about dinosaurs? But she put her finger to her lips and led me to the smaller of the two ponds, which was overgrown with reeds.

'You must promise to be very quiet so you don't scare him,' she said and I almost laughed. Being quiet was my speciality.

'He's called Amarelo. You'll see.'

We sat by the water's edge, and she mouthed, 'Wait.'

We stared into the pool for what felt like an eternity. My body began to cramp, but I was scared to move a muscle, in case I broke the spell. At last, a tiny black head with two beady, yellow eyes bobbed up on the surface of the water.

Maya held her hand up to say, *Don't move*. We held our breath. The creature climbed on to the shore less than a metre from her hand. It was silvery grey with a line of black spikes along its back, like a mini Stegosaurus, a big wide flat tail, which *swooshed* from side to side, and blotchy skin. But the most magnificent thing about it was its bright yellow belly, which made it seem as though it was filled with a fluorescent light. The creature seemed to belong to an entirely different, prehistoric world.

And as quickly as it appeared, it turned and disappeared below the surface of the water.

'The great crested newt,' Maya whispered. 'I call him Amarelo, because it means "yellow" in Portuguese – you know, because of his belly. He's extremely rare. Doesn't he look like a tiny dragon? Did you notice his feet?'

I shook my head, full of awe at what I'd seen.

'They are like tiny versions of the one that made your print. A dinosaur – or a dragon!'

Something happened then. My chest expanded. Words threatened to escape. But I didn't stop them, because I felt that I didn't have to. For the first time in ages, I wanted to speak.

'You love dragons, don't you?' I asked, raising an eyebrow and smiling. The question sounded dry and croaky in my throat, almost as if it didn't belong to me. But it worked! It had been five months, two weeks and six days since I'd said anything to anyone, but my voice still worked! I felt momentarily guilty that these first words weren't to Mum, or to Jomar, or Ravi, but when Maya smiled at me, I stopped worrying. And unlike with Mum, it wasn't a big deal. She just answered my question.

'Oh, yes,' she said seriously. 'I think they're incredible.'

I cleared my throat a couple of times. Words jostled excitedly inside me, awaiting their turn.

'Would you like to hear a story about one?' I asked. My voice was louder and clearer this time, and I found I was enjoying myself. Talking to Maya felt completely normal. And now that I'd started, there was so much I wanted to say.

'Always.'

'It's actually a legend. One which my grandpa told my dad, and he told me.'

We went to sit in the train carriage out of the wind and I continued talking, happy at the words pouring out of me. It was my favourite legend about the Wawel dragon, which I used to ask Dad to read over and over and over when I was younger, and which I listened to on my headphones at night before falling asleep. It sounded so much better in his voice, but I did my best.

'A long time ago, when King Krak ruled the lands, a dragon appeared in Kraków. He was a huge, fire-breathing creature with warty skin and evil yellow eyes. Nobody knew where he'd come from, but he settled in a cave under Wawel Castle and it turned out that he had an insatiable appetite. The townspeople brought him huge piles of pies, meat and cake. But he was still hungry.

The dragon was everywhere: in the scratch of his claws as he turned in his sleep, in the sparks from his nostrils that cut the night like lightning, in the smoke, which hung in the air like a dark cloud, heralding doom. But most of all, he was the fear of every inhabitant of the town, as they closed their shutters tight, barricaded their doors with sacks of flour, and burned incense, hoping that he would stay away. He didn't, of course.

The king decreed that he would bestow infinite wealth on whoever managed to rid the town of the dragon. A few daredevils came forward, but none of them returned from the dragon's lair. Both the king and his subjects had given up hope of rescue. It was obvious that Kraków would soon entirely run out of food.

One day, a poor farrier's apprentice named Skuba appeared at the court of Krak.

'My lord, I can defeat the dragon that torments us,' he said, bowing low to the king.

The knights laughed at him. The kinder among them warned him that far stronger people had failed in this quest and that he would be going to certain death.

Skuba listened, but he wasn't swayed. Soon,

everything was ready. He killed the finest ram he could find, stuffed it with sulphur and sewed it up. He slung it over his back and headed towards the dragon's cave. As silently as he could, he crept to the entrance, threw in the stuffed ram and ran away.

The dragon, attracted by the smell of fresh meat, devoured it. But the sulphur hidden inside made the dragon thirstier than ever before. He rushed towards the river and he drank and drank and drank. Onlookers said that he might drink the river dry. Suddenly there was a huge explosion. The dragon had drunk so much water that he'd ... burst. The ingenious Skuba became the hero of the town, and the king rewarded him handsomely.'

'No way,' said Maya, looking horrified. 'That's awful.'

'What is?'

'Skuba could have tried other ways to get rid of him. He didn't have to torture the dragon to death.'

I stared at her, puzzled.

'That's the part of the story that shocked you? Not the dragon terrorising everyone in the town?'

'He must have had a reason to. There's always a reason,' she replied.

'My dad used to say that the moral is to use your head to tackle problems.'

'True, but it's not so easy when you're scared. And the people in your story were petrified. That's probably why they did what they did. It doesn't make it right.'

'I hadn't thought about it like that before,' I admitted. 'But they're not real people. It's just a story – although a great one.'

'I didn't read many stories when I was younger,' said Maya. 'My avó read to me when I was small and she was the queen of stories. Or maybe a sorceress, because she would magic up exactly what I wanted to hear. She died when I was five. I loved her very much and I still think about her. People say you don't remember things from when you're that young, but I do. My parents are scientists – conservationists – and they've never been much into stories. They prefer hard facts. You're so lucky that your dad is interested in stories and that he still reads them to you.'

I wanted to tell her. I was very nearly ready. But it would be the first time that I would be saying it aloud to anyone, ever, and I panicked.

'Your parents have cool jobs, though,' I said, changing the subject. 'Is that why you moved here?'

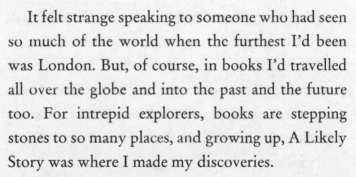

'Yeah, my dad's come to study the bee population. We're from Brazil, but we've lived in Iceland and Japan too. We travel a lot because of his work. He's mainly stationed at the research centre now. My sister's at university and my mum home-schools me.'

It felt strange speaking to someone who had seen so much of the world when the furthest I'd been was London. But, of course, in books I'd travelled all over the globe and into the past and the future too. For intrepid explorers, books are stepping stones to so many places, and growing up, A Likely Story was where I made my discoveries.

'What kinds of things have your parents worked on?' I asked.

'Mainly species at risk of extinction. In Iceland they were studying bowhead whales, and in Japan, a species of fruit bat. And here it's bees. They're looking into the conditions needed to stop them from becoming extinct.'

'Is that the kind of work that you want to do when you're older?'

'Oh,' she said, and went quiet. 'I don't think I'm clever enough. My older sister, Catia, is studying biology, so she might. She's super-intelligent.'

'But you know so much about all of this,' I said, motioning towards the marshes. 'I've lived here my whole life and I didn't know any of the stuff you've told me.'

'Ah, I find it interesting, that's all,' she said. 'Tell me about your dad's stories. Are there more?'

'Legends? I know a few others, sure. And if you want to see a place that's full of stories, there's somewhere perfect I can take you. Are you free on Saturday afternoon?'

'I can be.'

'Meet me here at four p.m. and I'll take you there.'

'OK,' she said, a smile lighting up her face. 'You know, you were so quiet when we met. I had no idea that you could be so talkative! I like it.'

I felt myself filling with a warm glow.

'What's your name?' she asked.

'Konrad. But everyone calls me Kon. Remember your watch this time. I'm not very good at reading the sun,' I said.

We both laughed, and I felt guilty for a millisecond for feeling so happy. But the guilt didn't hang around like it usually did.

This time it was replaced by excitement, because I knew that Maya would love A Likely Story.

# 6

I couldn't wait for Saturday afternoon. For the first time in months, I had something real to look forward to. I imagined Maya's face when I showed her the bookshop. I wasn't a book matchmaker like Dad, but I was certain that by asking her a few questions, I could find out the kinds of stories she'd want to dive into. Had she read all the Roald Dahls? What books did they have in the countries where she'd lived?

I was so preoccupied thinking about the books I'd recommend that I ignored Luke all Friday, even though he was being particularly annoying. In music, Mr Phillips set us the task of writing and performing our own song, and I overheard

Luke whispering to Noah, 'Let's do ours about the monkey man who lives by the sea.' I knew he meant me, but I didn't care. Instead, I thought how awesome Maya would be at this. She wouldn't even need backing music. Her own otherworldly song would blow everyone away.

But my good mood bubble burst on Saturday, when Mum insisted we go to Alf's. Before she'd asked Stephen to take on more shifts, she would work on Saturdays and I had my routine. I would sleep in until at least ten. Then, I would get up for breakfast and spend ages perfecting my CHEEK-y sandwich, which Dad had introduced me to when I was little.

It's a delicious mix of chicken (roasted), ham (ideally the thicker variety), egg (hard-boiled and sliced), Edam cheese and ketchup.

Today, Mum was in the kitchen with her coffee and paper, but I decided to carry on as usual.

I peered in the fridge and struck gold. She'd done the shopping. I got two slices of bread and put them on the worktop. I slathered them in butter. There was even a ready-cooked chicken.

I was about to put two eggs in a pan to boil when Mum looked up and asked what I was doing and my Saturday morning routine was ruined.

'Kon, I thought we might go to Alf's, you know, make a day of it? Maybe we could finally get you some new trainers.'

I wondered why Mum thought that was a good idea, when we were supposed to be saving money, with the bookshop doing so badly. The prospect of going into town filled me with anxiety. It might mean bumping into Mum's friends, who'd try to speak to me, and avoiding kids from school.

I felt completely differently on the beach. Calmer and more myself. I'd realised yesterday, that talking to Maya wasn't like talking to anyone else, and I wasn't ready to speak to other people.

My shoulders tensed at the thought of the trip, but I got dressed and followed Mum out of the door, trying my best to seem cheerful. We spent ages searching for a place to park, which put Mum in a foul mood. Eventually we found a space. I tried to smile when I accidentally caught her eye – I could see that she was determined we'd enjoy ourselves.

The first stop was the fudge shop near the cathedral. I used to love going there. Mrs Higgs, who ran it, knew Dad from when *he* was little. She always let me taste the new flavours, even the weird ones, like watermelon (gross) or raspberry liquorice (doubly gross) or salty lemon sorbet (surprisingly nice).

I really couldn't face going in today, but Mum was on a mission. The minute I saw Mrs Higgs' face, I wanted to walk straight out again.

'Oh, how lovely to see you,' she said awkwardly. 'How are you both doing?' she continued, in that hushed voice I'd heard so much of lately.

'Fine,' said Mum breezily. 'Now, we thought today we might get...'

'You know, I cried all evening when I heard,' said Mrs Higgs, staring at me. 'I still remember the day that he came in here with your nana. They were my first customers and, you know, he looked just like you do now. He had the chocolate fudge. Back then we didn't have that many flavours. But he said to me—'

'I think we'll have the salted caramel,' said Mum, cutting her off.

'Of course,' said Mrs Higgs, as if someone had thrown a bucket of water over her. 'Sorry, I didn't mean to ramble on. I'm sure you have had a hard— Anyway, do you want to try any of my new flavours? It might cheer you up a bit.'

I shook my head.

So we bought the salted caramel fudge and Mum rushed us out of the shop.

'Some people can't feel the room, can they?' she muttered under her breath. 'Come on, let's find you some trainers. I might look for some tennis shoes for myself. I said I'd do a bit more exercise.'

I wandered around the shoe shop, lingering in the high-tops section. There were some limited-edition ones with graffiti slogans, but they cost more than a hundred pounds and there was no way we could afford them. I have huge feet for my age, so I have to buy trainers from the adult section, which means paying more.

I spotted a reduced pair in blue and white, which Mum might be able to afford. The display model was even in my size. I took off my dirty trainers. They were in a state. On the left one, the fabric had already torn at the big toe. I slid the new ones on and for a second, I was transformed. I wasn't Konrad any more. I was an intrepid space traveller who had landed on a new planet. I was about to call Mum over to show her, when I heard her talking to somebody.

'Hannah! It's been ages. How are you?'

My heart sank. Hannah was Luke's mum. The last thing I needed was to see Luke on a non-school day. But there he was, nosing around by the footballs with Noah.

'It's so sad that they don't hang out any more,' Hannah whispered so loudly that I bet most of the shop heard.

'Oh?' said Mum. 'I didn't realise. Well, Kon keeps himself to himself these days. And I've been so busy with the bookshop...'

I went to put the trainer back on the display before Luke spotted me, but he turned at that precise moment.

'Trying to get back to civilisation, monkey boy?' he said, smirking.

'Yeah, you can try,' Noah added, 'but no amount

of designer gear will change who you are. We'll still smell you from a mile off.'

Red fury flooded my vision. I tried to think about the bookshop, Maya, anything other than the rage that was going to engulf me.

'Kon, darling,' said Mum, coming towards us with Hannah. 'Are those the ones you've chosen? They're not very practical, are they? How will you play football in those? Is that how much they cost? Extortionate. Come on, let's find something more sensible.'

'Oh, yes, sensible is better,' said Luke sweetly.

I tried to shut my eyes and block out their voices, but I couldn't. What was worse was that Luke would replay this scene word for word at school to anyone who would listen. It was too much. I shouldn't ever have agreed to come.

The waves in my stomach mounted. Words erupted. 'Leave me alone!' I screamed. 'Why can't you all leave me alone?'

I saw Mum's shocked face and ran out of the shop, flying blindly down the road, not looking where I was going. There was a queue of people outside the waffle van in the square and I almost collided with them.

I felt a firm hand on my shoulder and a voice saying, 'It's OK. Slow down. It's OK.' I'd forgotten what a fast runner Mum is.

Ten minutes later we were sitting on opposite sides of the booth at Alf's and she was staring at me. It felt like the first time in months that she'd met my eye and I forced myself to look back at her. It was only then I noticed how different she seemed. Her blue jumper was much looser on her than before, and her face was pale. I felt an urge to slide over into her booth and hug her tightly. I was about to get up, when she said:

'I shouldn't have made you come into town today. I'm sorry. I thought it would make a change from sitting at home, feeling miserable. But you spoke, Kon!' she said. 'It's so good to hear your voice, even if you are angry.'

I nodded. I hoped she didn't expect me to say anything more. I didn't want to.

She took my hands between hers. 'Is there something going on with Luke?' she asked.

I should have told her months ago, when he'd first started calling me names. Now it was so far down the line, I didn't know where to begin.

'You can tell me, Kon. I can have a word with Hannah, maybe that would —'

I shook my head and looked away.

We ate our cod and chips, and Mum tried to make conversation by telling me funny stories about her old clients from the salon, and I smiled because I knew she wanted me to. But pretending was exhausting, and I wanted to go home.

I hopped out of the car as soon as we were in the drive and started walking towards the beach. I'd managed to take about three steps when Mum wound down the window, surprised.

'I love you,' I said, and quickly turned around before I could see her cry.

7

Maya was waiting for me by the train carriage. I could see her a mile off, and my mood instantly changed.

Today she was wearing a bright blue dress with huge yellow sunflowers on it. It skimmed the ground as she walked. She had a blazer over the top, and she was wearing shoes instead of her mucky wellingtons. When they poked out from the bottom of her dress, I saw that they were high-top trainers, like the ones I'd seen earlier. Except hers were white with multi-coloured biro all over them.

'Nice trainers.'

'My favourite song lyrics – they travel with me everywhere. So where are *we* going?'

I led her down Meadowfield Lane, which ran

behind Ocean Drive, then round the back of the cathedral to avoid the high street. It was pretty far, but luckily Maya was a fast walker. She began humming a tune I recognised. The song she'd been singing the first time I heard her on the beach.

'The way you sing – it's really unusual. In a good way,' I said to her. 'You know, Mr Phillips, our music teacher, would be totally amazed if he heard you. I bet he'd want you to do the solos in all our school plays.'

She didn't say anything at first, and I wondered whether I'd embarrassed her.

'Nobody's ever said that to me before,' she said finally in a strange voice. 'Do you honestly think so? It's sometimes lonely at home, especially when Mum needs to work. I would love to come to your school, Kon.'

'Well, I think you should ask your parents. Tell them we have an awesome music department. And obviously you'd already have one friend – me.'

'That's true,' she said, laughing.

'Here it is,' I said, as we arrived outside A Likely Story. My heart was hammering as I took in the window. Everything was different. Stephen must have changed the display to make it spring-like. It was filled with books featuring bunnies and chicks, and a bright range of titles in the colours and shape of a rainbow. The sign for the book matchmaker was still there and my breath caught in my throat. There was no way that I could go in. But then in the depths of my mind, I heard Dad's voice: 'Sometimes things are tough, my intrepid explorer. But you need to let the lights bleed into the darks.' I turned the handle.

'Ah, there you are,' said Stephen. 'Admiring my handiwork, I see. Who's this?' he asked, smiling at Maya.

'Hello. I'm a new friend,' she said, introducing herself. I was grateful because my voice faltered and all I could do was nod.

'Great to meet you. So, I guess you haven't been here before?'

'No. First time,' said Maya. 'I'm excited. What are these?' she asked, gesturing to the rainbow titles.

'Oh, it's a selection of new books I've picked out. This is a brilliant new story for younger children.

It's about the different shapes and sizes that families come in. And this one's about a bunny who doesn't want to go to bed.'

'Ah, my avó would read me a similar story when I was little,' said Maya. 'It helped me get to sleep. And what's that?' she asked, pointing to a familiar-looking book showing a blond boy standing on a planet.

'That's a new edition of *The Little Prince*. It's actually one of my favourite books ever. Have you read it?'

'No. What's it about?'

'That's a good question. It's about so many things! There's a prince who visits different planets. He feels lonely and wants to find out more about love, the universe and everything in it.'

'It sounds amazing,' said Maya seriously. 'I think I would like it.'

'I'm sure you would. Pick up a copy for yourself from me. And I hope you like the bookshop too. It's a pretty special place. I'll be sad to leave it. It's not big but to me it's always been filled with a little bit of magic. Have a browse. Enjoy it. Kon, there's a pile of books at the back with your name on it.'

'Thank you for the copy of *The Little Prince*! And Kon's pile of books sounds intriguing,' added Maya on my behalf.

'You remember how to lock up, don't you?' said Stephen, smiling at me.

I nodded.

'OK, then. Well, I'd better be off. I have dinner waiting for me at home,' he said, switching the sign on the door to *Closed*. Give your mum my love.'

He waved goodbye, and there we were, alone with the familiar smell of old wood and print.

Maya's eyes widened as she looked around. She took in the book-lined walls, the cosy armchairs, fairy lights in the windows and the old counter. I hoped she saw it as the special place that I knew it was.

'Wow. So you're friends with the owner? In Sao Paulo, my avó knew the owner of the bookshop in our district. You had to climb this tiny, winding staircase to get to the top and there was a cafe too, with views over the whole town. My avó would spend ages browsing and we would read together on the balcony when the weather was nice. I haven't been back to a bookshop since, not properly.'

'This is my dad's,' I said.

'Your dad's? Was that your dad, then?'

'No, no – that's Stephen,' I said, feeling myself grow hot. The last thing I wanted was Maya to feel sorry for me. I could have avoided answering her directly, but I didn't.

I lowered my eyes. 'He died,' I said. 'At the start of November last year. He used to run it and Stephen worked for him. But now Mum plans to sell it. She's struggling to run it the way he used to.'

There. I'd said it.

I felt her hand touch mine and squeeze briefly.

'Ah,' she said. 'OK.' She didn't say, 'I'm sorry,' or, 'How awful,' or any of the things that I'd heard so many times and made me never want to say anything to anyone ever again.

Maya smiled a half-smile. 'So, where are we going to start?'

'Start what?'

'Start reading!'

'Oh, well. Do you see that sign over there about the book matchmaker? That's what my dad used to be. He thought that he could match everyone with the perfect book. Actually, that's another thing he used to tell me. That for every reader there is a character in a book somewhere that matches them almost exactly. It's just a case of finding them.'

'But that's impossible. Think how many books there are in the world. There's no way you could read them all,' she said. 'Even if you were a super-speed reader.'

'It sounds unlikely, I know. But the books that you're meant to find have a way of finding you,' I said confidently.

'Well, have you found yours yet?'

'No, but I've got years, haven't I? I might not find my character until I'm twenty-nine, or sixty-one or a hundred.'

'Hmmm,' said Maya, taking off her shoes and blazer and putting them carefully by the till.

I must have given her a weird look because she explained, 'I need to get comfortable. And sometimes even my favourite songs need a break from me.' She straightened out the laces on her trainers, to show the words written in between.

'Hey, I reckon that your character would definitely be a singer,' I said, thinking hard. 'I haven't read anything with singers in recently. But maybe we can find something together? Let me have a look.' I switched on the computer.

I typed *Singing* into the search bar. Loads of books came up straight away about the technique of learning how to sing. I filtered the results by clicking on fiction. The list was long, but they were all for little kids. None of them would be right for Maya.

'Don't worry,' she said. 'I don't think my character would be a singer. I would be someone in the background, observing.'

'What? Why?'

Her eyebrows knitted together. I could tell that she didn't know how to answer.

'Because I'm not a person who *does* things,' she said eventually. 'I've never been good at school. It took me a long time to learn to read, and I still get letters muddled. Maybe that's why I haven't read that many books myself.'

I sensed that it had taken a lot for her to tell me this and I was glad that she had.

'You speak two languages,' I pointed out. 'That's incredible.'

'Yeah, but that's because I heard them when I was growing up. My mum spoke to me in Portuguese and Dad spoke English. Anyway, let's talk about you,' she said, quickly changing the subject. 'You must have an idea about which section your book might be in.'

'Well, yeah. This is where I'd like to find myself,' I said, taking her over to the Endangered Species section. 'But these are all factual books, so not exactly, although I'd love to be one of those authors uncovering new science, like Jim Jacobsen, the dinosaur expert. What a cool way to spend your time.'

'Look at this,' said Maya, picking up a book called *The Hidden World of Reptiles*. 'I bet Amarelo is in here somewhere.'

While she searched for her newt, I consulted *Dinosaur Tracks and other Fossil Footprints of Europe* and took out my phone to look at my print. I flicked past the Triceratops chapter, as I knew that they had far too many toes. The feet of

Iguanodons had three prongs, but the footprint in the book had much wider claws than the one I found.

I looked up the Baryonyx to see whether the print could have belonged to him, but it was different to the footprint shape drawn in the book. Then I paused on a double-page spread dedicated to the Megalosaurus. This seemed more likely, but there was still something about the width of each prong that didn't look quite right.

None of the footprints in the book matched the one I'd found. The mystery thickened.

'Here he is!' said Maya happily, pointing to a picture of a newt that looked exactly like Amarelo. 'It says that great crested newts have been around for approximately forty million years. Wow! I had no idea.'

She shut the book and started to explore the other shelves.

My disappointment at not finding my fossil was quickly forgotten. Being in the bookshop with Maya was fun. I was rediscovering the magic that Dad always spoke about.

She found the Roald Dahl collection and laughed at Quentin Blake's illustrations for *The BFG*.

'See, he's taking her dream,' she said, pointing to a picture of Sophie and looking so delighted that I immediately took a copy and put it to one side for her.

I read her some of my favourite bits from *Northern Lights* and she read the opening of some adult books because she liked the titles. She thought that *I Know Why the Caged Bird Sings* might list all the reasons on the first page and that *Catch 22* was mysterious, because so many other catches had come before it.

'Why is the twenty-second one special?' she asked, her eyebrows raised. 'Don't you want to find out?'

Then I spotted my pile of books in the corner. I scanned the spines and knew what they were even before I read the note on top, scrawled in Mum's handwriting: *To take home for Kon*.

'These are yours to keep?' asked Maya appreciatively. It was a mix of stories I loved when I was younger, a couple of books from the dinosaur section and a few titles I'd picked up when I was last at the shop, meaning to read them, but forgetting to take them home. I wondered how Mum knew.

'Maybe I could borrow some of these after you've finished?' asked Maya hopefully.

'Yeah, for sure.'

'But what's this one?' she asked, pulling out a book from the middle of the pile. 'Look at it – it's beautiful.'

She handed it to me, and I ran my fingers over the silky green cover. My heart stopped. Tiny footprints, embossed in gold, stamped around the edges of the cover, shaped just like the one I'd found. I turned the book over, checking the spine, but strangely there was no title. This book wasn't new, like the others. It looked very old, as if it had come from a distant past, when dragons and magic might have existed. When I finally dared to open it, the thin, yellow paper crackled beneath my fingertips and gave out a sweet, musty smell.

I turned carefully to the title page where there was a picture of a dragon. It was so detailed and intricate that I could see every muscle in the dragon's body.

It had magnificent, gleaming, fiery scales and vast, sweeping wings. His yellow eyes sent goosebumps down my spine. This wasn't just any dragon.

'Hey! Maya, it's the dragon of Wawel Castle! From the legend I told you. It's the one that my dad used to read to me.' I ran my finger across the green text. The ink shimmered as I read:

*A long time ago, when King Krak ruled the lands, a dragon appeared in Kraków. He was a huge, fire-breathing creature with warty skin and evil yellow eyes. Nobody knew where he'd come from, but he settled in a cave under Wawel Castle and it turned out that he had an insatiable appetite.*

I flipped the page, savouring every word of the story, somehow seeing it come to life like never before. Maybe it was the richly coloured illustrations, or the print that looked like old-fashioned writing. As I read, I had a peculiar feeling that the light around me was changing, but all I wanted was to get to the end.

'Konrad?' It was Maya's voice, but it didn't sound like her – cheerful and carefree. It was small and shaky and scared.

I glanced up. She was still there next to me. I was still holding the book. There were shelves of other books around us, but we weren't in Dad's bookshop any more. We were somewhere else entirely.

# 8

At first, I thought that I had passed out. There was no other explanation. I'd come round any moment and everything would be as before.

I didn't dare speak in case it made the situation worse and slowed down the process of me waking up. But Maya was growing more and more frantic.

'Konrad! What's happened? Where are we?' she asked over and over in her tiny voice. Her blue flowery dress had gone. Instead, she was wearing what appeared to be a brown sack with long sleeves, and a white apron over the top. Her wild hair was tied into two neat plaits. My panic mounted. What was going on?

I stared down at my hands. The green silky cover of the book gave off an unearthly glow. I noticed with disbelief that the footprints I'd seen only moments ago were fading before my eyes. I flicked through the pages. The words were gone.

'Maya! Look at the book! The pages are blank. The story has disappeared!'

'What? Kon, what's happened to us?' She was crying now.

I looked up. The room was cast in a half-shadow, the light seeping through a narrow window. We must be partly underground, because a pair of feet could be seen walking by. The floor beneath us was stone, the ceiling was low and there was something about the rough wooden table in the corner, and the melted candle in a plain iron holder, that gave me the distinct feeling that we weren't in the present day.

The walls and every available surface were covered in books, but they were nothing like those in A Likely Story. These had leather covers, or the same strange, silky material as the book I was holding. They were haphazardly arranged in piles, as if whoever had left them hadn't had time to put them on the shelves properly, with the spines facing outwards.

Suddenly a distant growl broke through the dusty darkness, like an approaching storm. The walls began to shake around us, the books on the shelves trembled and the growl turned into a thunderous roar that I could feel in every fibre of my being. Next to me, Maya fell to the floor with her hands over her head.

'It's an earthquake! Duck!' she cried. Her hand reached and pulled me down next to her.

Panic paralysed me and even though the noise had subsided, I couldn't move. With a creak, the trapdoor in the ceiling opened, spilling a pool of light on to the floor. Maya screamed.

'Is all well?' a woman's voice called. She stepped down the ladder, holding a candle like the one on the table. 'You must be Konrad and Maya.'

She had blonde hair tied in a ponytail, blue eyes and pale, freckled skin. She looked about the same age as Mum and didn't seem the slightest bit shocked to see us.

'Didn't they pass on the message that I was going to collect you from the monastery? I would have come on horseback. It's much safer in the current times. You poor things. Did Peter let you in? You must have been frightened to death when you heard the noise. I ran all the way from the bakery. I know I shouldn't have, but it was instinct. Perhaps I could sense that you'd arrived and wanted to make sure you were safe?'

'Safe?'

'Anyhow, he's left now. I heard him going back up the hill. Hopefully he'll stay there until nightfall, like yesterday. We must remember what the king said: not to be scared, even if he's close. Especially if he's close. He can smell our fear and it unleashes fury within him.'

I stared at her.

'Who can?' I asked carefully.

'Goodness, I'm sorry. I'm speaking too fast. I meant Yellow Eye. I was talking about the dragon.'

I croaked in disbelief. Yellow Eye! In some versions of the legend about the Wawel dragon, this was the name he was known by. My brain had conjured the story and now I was dreaming about it. But why? And how had the dream come to life? I didn't understand.

'I'm so thankful that you've come to work for me. I have everything set up for your lodging,' the woman continued. 'I know it seems like madness, but we need to continue working, despite everything that's going on, or maybe because of it. We can't let him destroy any more books.'

She shuffled over to a set of shelves without any books on them. They were covered in rolls of something that looked like paper but had a strange texture and jagged edges.

'Barely enough room to move in here,' she muttered. 'Why did I ever volunteer to take the king's books?'

She picked up three rolls and a couple of other objects that I didn't recognise.

'Come on. Let's go upstairs and I can show you what's what,' she said.

I glanced at Maya. In the faint light she was so pale that I thought she might pass out.

'Where are we?' she asked weakly.

The woman gave her a worried look. She raised the candle to Maya's face and her expression relaxed a little.

'May I?'

She touched Maya's forehead with the back of her hand.

'Are you sick, Maya? Your head feels warm. When Peter comes, we'll get him to fetch Dr Wilski. I'm sure he can visit us within the hour.'

'But where are we?' Maya repeated, her voice shaking.

'You're with me, Teresa Bem, the scribe. You've come from Balice Farm to help me with the house while I've been set this project by the king. And this is Konrad. He arrived on the same day from the monastery scriptorium. He's helping me copy out all the books. You know this, but right now you're clearly not yourself, so we need to perk you up. Let's start by getting you upstairs.'

I was frantically trying to make sense of everything that I'd heard. If this was some weird nightmare, then why was Maya so scared? She obviously felt the same as me.

I took her by the hand and led her to the ladder – Maya first, then me, and last, the woman called Teresa.

We emerged in a large, cosy-looking room, with a roaring fire, and three chairs around a table.

At one end of the room was a smaller table painted white, with a row of open books on it. Except they didn't resemble the books I knew. The pages were leathery, and the text looked as if it had been written by hand with one of those posh calligraphy pens that I'd once seen Luke's mum use for his party invitations. But Teresa's writing implement was a large quill which was balanced on top of an ink pot. In the light of the candle, her hands were completely stained with black and gold.

An odd, sweet smell hung in the air. On either side of the doorway were incense sticks, like the kind that Mum used to burn at Ocean Drive when she was having a bath.

'Peter should be here soon,' she said. 'But in the meantime, I've left your pies to cool, so we may as well have dinner while we're waiting. Maya, dear, do you feel well enough to eat? It's beef and potato. It would do you good to get your strength up.'

The minute Teresa went to the stove at the other end of the room, I turned to Maya.

'You remember?' I whispered. 'It's not just me? You remember. We were both in the bookshop and suddenly – I don't know what happened... And now we're here.'

'The green book. You opened the green book.'

'Yes! The book about the dragon of Wawel Castle.'

'We're in it.'

'I know... But how? Are we dreaming? And why have the pages of the book gone blank? I think it must be some kind of clue, but I have no idea what it means.'

'No! We can't be. We can't both be. It doesn't make sense. How do we get back?' She was crying and I felt like the worst person in the entire world.

I held her tightly. 'I promise I'll get us back. I don't know how yet, but I'll find a way. It's my fault, and I'll make it right.' I tried to sound confident but a feeling of helplessness washed over me.

'Sorry I'm late,' said a man's voice at the door. My heart leaped. There was something about it that sounded very familiar.

'Peter! Could you go and see if the doctor's in? The young girl's not well.'

'Of course. I'll be back in a moment.'

'Who was that?' I asked. I felt a rush of terror and excitement all at once.

'Oh, it's Peter. He lives next door and runs the bakery. I'm sure he'll be glad to meet you. Makes a change from the two of us bickering all the time.'

She'd barely finished setting the table, when the door opened, and two men appeared. One was elderly, with greying hair and a bristly moustache. He carried what looked like a wooden box of tools, but as he came closer, I saw that it was filled with tiny bottles and glass vials. The second man was tall, with brown, curly hair. His trousers and wool jacket were covered in a fine smattering of white flour. He smelled of something sweet and homely, and when he unwrapped the parcel he was carrying, there was fresh bread inside.

Something about him filled me with calm. The panic was still there, but it had shrunk. He raised his hand in greeting.

'This young lady is the patient?' Dr Wilski asked.

'Yes, I'm —' Maya broke off, as if she wasn't sure what to say.

'Right,' said the doctor, sitting down on a stool opposite her. 'Please allow me to examine you. What's the malady here?'

'Faintness and confusion,' said Teresa. 'Only natural in the current circumstances. I dare say that most of us are not feeling ourselves.'

'Well, yes. Quite,' the doctor muttered. He looked carefully into Maya's eyes. Then he held his thumbs on her inside wrists and counted under his breath. Finally, he checked her forehead and seemed satisfied.

'What's your name?' he asked.

'Maya.'

'Age?'

'Twelve.'

'And whose house is this?' he asked.

'Teresa's,' said Maya.

I was relieved that some of the initial panic seemed to have left her.

'A slight fever,' the doctor announced. 'Your pulse is a little fast. Mix two spoons of dried coriander with a hot broth before bed. You should be restored to your former self by tomorrow. If the symptoms persist, please call on me again.'

'Thank you, Dr Wilski. We are indebted,' Teresa said, pressing two gold coins into his palm.

'I won't take it,' he protested. 'Peter here has done more than enough to feed my family over the past weeks. I don't know how we'd have survived without him.' He had another patient to get to so made to leave, but before he stepped into the street, he turned anxiously both ways to make sure the coast was clear.

Teresa, who had put our pies back on the stove to warm, now placed them on the table. They smelled delicious and I surprised myself by how hungry I was. Peter motioned me to sit next to him.

Maya hesitated only for a moment before taking a bite. I could tell that she was ravenous too. I devoured a spoonful of sauce that had oozed out of the pastry. It felt like ages since I'd last eaten. My mouth was filled with delicious hot goodness and for a split-second I forgot where I was.

'You don't know how glad I am that you both made it here safely,' Peter said, and his voice was warm and gentle. 'Have you heard the latest about what's been happening? The beast escaped his lair this afternoon. The fence that we'd built around the cave didn't help. Forty men risked their lives during the early hours of the morning, putting it up while he was asleep, only for it to be torn down in an instant.'

'I can't say I'm shocked,' Teresa said. 'They've tried so many things. It'll soon be a month that he's been here. I honestly hope that the king will come to his senses and order us all to flee.'

'He won't,' said Peter. 'Everything we own is in Kraków. And it's not as though the problem will disappear if we leave. The beast will likely come into the forest after us. Notice that he hasn't actually hurt any of us. Not deliberately, at least.'

'Not yet. But he's not satisfied until we deposit practically every item of food we've produced outside his cave. Admit it, you're running out of flour. You haven't said it, but I know.'

'We're not doing well,' said Peter sadly, breaking his pie into tiny pieces to make it last longer. 'But who is? We need to keep going. There's a way out of this. We just need to find it.'

'We need more support from our leaders,' said

Teresa, pouring warm milk into chipped earthenware mugs. 'We need someone to sort the situation out once and for all. This is madness – spending our days producing food and expecting incense to ward off a dragon.'

'Hey, we shouldn't be talking like this on your first day,' said Peter, checking himself. 'We're terrible hosts. I apologise. We're happy that you've come to help Teresa. The last thing that we want is for the beast to destroy our books. Where would we be without them? Can you imagine a world without myths? Without stories? Nothing to pass on to the people who come after us?'

'It would be awful,' I agreed. I had a sudden flashback of sitting with Dad in A Likely Story and discussing the importance of books. 'Stories are a part of us all,' he'd said. 'They've been around since the beginning of time.'

'It was Peter who first went to the king to ask whether we could recreate the books that had been destroyed,' said Teresa, with a note of admiration. 'And we got the agreement from the monastery to get Konrad to help me. Father Stefan said that you were the best student in the scriptorium,' she said, looking at me.

'But … what happened?' I immediately wished that I could take the question back. I was giving myself away. Teresa didn't seem to notice.

'Didn't Father Stefan tell you? The most precious books were taken from the royal collection to get them as far as possible from the dragon. With Yellow Eye's cave being directly below the castle, the king thought it a real danger to have such precious volumes so close. And he was right to be concerned. I think it was the carelessness of the men employed to move the books that caused this,' she said boldly.

'It might be so,' said Peter. 'But nobody could have expected it. The men left the books stacked outside the castle entrance in bundles, thinking they would be collected on horseback that evening before the dragon woke. That's when Yellow Eye usually goes for a wander round the town. But the dragon rose early, and he must have thought the parcels contained food. He was so angry that he ripped them apart with his teeth and burned them with his flame. They couldn't be saved.'

'Luckily, being an official scribe, Teresa has some of the early editions here. She's working on *The Book of Ancient Legends*. She needs to create at least twenty copies to make sure that the stories are truly safe for future generations.'

'And you'll play a big part in helping me achieve that, I hope,' said Teresa, looking at me.

'Wow,' said Maya. I could tell that, like me, she was astounded by the task I'd been set.

'I've been so looking forward to seeing you,' said Peter, smiling.

'Me too,' I found myself replying. And the strangest thing was that I meant it.

A growl broke through the silence and I was brought back to reality. We held our breath. Peter was sitting super-straight and still, his finger to his lips.

'It's nothing. Must have been a dog. It wasn't the sort of noise the beast usually makes.'

Maya stared at me pleadingly and I tried to transmit a message to say it was going to be OK. I would make it OK.

'Right, I'll be off. Early start tomorrow,' said Peter. 'Thank you for the delicious meal.'

And before I could say anything else, he was out in the streets of medieval Kraków, where there were no cars, phones or computers, where people got around by horse and cart, and where a hungry, fire-breathing, book-destroying dragon roamed the land, eating anything he could lay his claws on.

9

I woke to a clunking sound, and in those first moments before opening my eyes, I was certain that it was Mum in the kitchen making me pancakes before school.

But then the dragon, Peter and Teresa came back to me and my heart started pounding. How had I arrived in the house of a scribe in the Polish city of Kraków more than eight hundred years ago?

When I sat up, I was in a tiny loft which Teresa had said would be my bedroom. It was cramped but cosy, which in normal circumstances I could get used to. There was a bed with a hay-stuffed mattress, a couple of rows of books, a desk with a chair, and a window looking out on to the street. Maya had been given a space downstairs with Teresa in a room off the main living area.

I peered through the dusty glass of the window. It must have been early, because there weren't many people around in the streets. I saw carts filled with vegetables being pulled up a steep hill. A woman struggled under a pile of laundry, and a group of men in official-looking red uniforms knocked on a door further down the road.

There was something about the scene that bothered me and I couldn't put my finger on what it was. But the intrepid explorer in me surveyed the street again, taking in every detail. The white stone houses with their large beams, leaning into each other as they mounted the hill. Some painted wooden eggs on a window sill, a forgotten Easter decoration. The laundress and the soldiers. Momentarily all was quiet. It had rained overnight, and there were puddles everywhere. Only then did I notice their odd shape. The water on the cobbled street lay in trenches made by the wheels of many carts. Hundreds, possibly thousands of them, had worn away at the stone, moulding and polishing it.

This must have once, maybe not so long ago, been a main thoroughfare. I couldn't imagine that now. Kraków had become a ghost town.

The sound of a trumpet from behind the house surprised me. It continued for what felt like ages and then stopped as abruptly as it had started. It was as if the person playing had given up midway.

Suddenly, I remembered about the strange green book. Last night, I'd stayed up until I knew that Teresa was asleep before going down to the basement to get it. I'd decided to store it safely under my new bed, because it was obvious that it held some important clues. Even the vanishing text had to mean something. I kneeled on the dusty floor and pulled it out, my hands shaking. I could tell straight away that it looked different to yesterday. There was still no text on the front cover, but the border of gold dragon footprints had returned. I stared at them in disbelief and then turned to the first page.

*A long time ago, when King Krak ruled the lands, a dragon appeared in Kraków. He was a huge, fire-breathing creature with warty skin and evil yellow eyes. Nobody knew where he'd come from, but he settled in a cave under Wawel Castle and it turned out that he had an insatiable appetite.*

I reread those sentences – which I knew by heart – over and over. I ran my finger over them. How had those words come back?

At the sound of footsteps, I quickly closed the book and put it back under the bed.

'Ah, you're finally awake,' said Teresa, startling me. She stood at the trapdoor with a pile of clothes. She handed me grey sack trousers and a white shirt, this time with no collar. It was less formal than what I'd found myself wearing yesterday.

'It's nearly nine o'clock,' she said. 'You've slept for twelve hours. Maya's up and she's feeling a lot better. Your breakfast is ready downstairs.'

As I stepped down the ladder, a delicious, milky smell filled the air. Teresa spooned something thick and gloopy from the pot that she had balanced on the stove into two earthenware bowls. She handed me a spoon and went back to her desk. I felt a pang of guilt. It was obvious that she'd been hard at work for hours.

I dipped my spoon into the thick mixture and tasted it on the tip of my tongue. It was grainy and sweet at the same time – some kind of porridge. Maya was cleaning the stove and gave me a look that implied we needed to talk. I tried to communicate with my eyes that I understood, and I'd find a good time.

'Today, Maya, you mustn't overexert yourself,' said Teresa. 'But I was hoping you could help Konrad and I with the page cutting. It's a rather delicate process and it might require the three of us.'

Maya nodded, but I could tell that she was freaking out like I was. Surely, it wouldn't take long for Teresa to realise that neither of us belonged here.

As soon as I'd finished eating, we went over

to the table and studied what Teresa was doing. I felt as though I was watching a dangerous science experiment in one of our school labs, which I'd have to recreate myself, barely understanding what needed to be done.

'Regretfully, we have little space here,' said Teresa. 'But we will have to make do. Be as careful as you can with the paper. We have a limited supply, and as you can imagine it's difficult to put in new orders in the present times.'

She handed me a long, thin metal ruler, and something that resembled a pencil, but without its wooden outer layer. Then she laid out a huge piece of cream-coloured paper in front of us and stroked it proudly.

'Such high quality,' she muttered. 'Now the page measurements that we're going by are fourteen fingers by eight,' she said, pointing at the marks on the ruler. 'I always mark out the corners with my stylus.' I realised that she was talking about the pencil-like object. 'I don't know how you usually work, but I make a faint line so that it can be easily covered by the ink border. Keep the pages close to each other, so that as little as possible is wasted in the cutting process.' Within moments, a faint grid had appeared at the top of Teresa's sheet.

'You continue marking out the pages for a minute,' she said to us, 'and I'll take the last of my work over there, so that I can finish my book. Then you can use my manuscript as your template, and we'll be up and running.'

She moved her piles of pages on to a smaller table closer to the stove and sat down. I looked over at Maya. I expected her to be staring back at me cluelessly, but she was biting her tongue in concentration and peering at the ruler with its strange markings. I couldn't believe that they measured things with their fingers. I couldn't even remember the numbers Teresa had mentioned. I stifled a nervous laugh.

Maya put the ruler on the giant piece of paper, careful not to crease it, and she boldly made a dot in the top left-hand corner with the stylus and another directly below. I watched, amazed, as she made a grid like Teresa's. I stared at my own blank piece of paper with panic. Noticing that Teresa was absorbed in her own work, Maya quickly drew the same grid on my paper. She finished just as Teresa walked over.

'Impressive,' she said, looking pleased. 'Maya, you are talented. You must help with the books from now on.'

She turned to me. 'Do you usually cut each page before starting or divide it into strips and separate the individual pages at the end?'

'Erm, strips.'

'I'm pleased. That's how I work too. It's so much easier if we use the same method.' She took a tiny sharp pocketknife and said, 'Allow me, please. It's because it's quite a specific blade. You need to know its quirks, otherwise you can go very wrong.'

'Of course,' I replied, relieved.

We watched as she gently pressed the knife into the paper and it glided smoothly across the horizontal line Maya had drawn. Soon, the table was filled with strips of paper, each with five 'pages' drawn on them.

'Splendid,' said Teresa, clapping her hands together. 'Now for the exciting part. I want you to start with the gold borders of the pages and the illustrations. It's quite an unusual order of doing things, but Father Stefan told me that you're good at drawing. The final stage will be adding the text.'

I studied the completed 'books' that she'd carried over. They didn't yet have a spine, so they were collections of pages. Gently, I lifted the cover off one of the piles and gazed at what was inside. The writing was large and loopy, each letter so precise that it looked as if it could have been typed. There wasn't a single splodge of ink, or smudge or mistake to show that the book had been created by hand. It was obviously an art. The borders were the least complicated part of the design, a series of gold lines finished with a flourish. If I concentrated hard, I could just about copy it.

Teresa must have noticed me admiring her books, because she said, 'We are lucky to be in this trade. I feel like I'm always leaving a trace of myself behind for future readers to find. There is a kind of magic that goes into making a book.'

'Are you any good at illustration?' I whispered to Maya when Teresa disappeared to the basement to fetch more ink.

'I can try,' she said, and managed a slight smile. 'At least I know the subject.'

She was right. The drawings were mainly of animals. There was even a creature that looked like a lizard. I flicked through the other book. One seemed to be of a castle that had been stormed by mice. Another showed a golden duck swimming to the edge of a pond and speaking to a man. The vivid green, red and gold pictures suddenly reminded me of the book of legends that Dad always read to me. I was certain that very similar ones had appeared there.

'It doesn't matter if there are slight differences between the drawings,' said Teresa, reappearing. 'Every artist has their own style. As long as they bring the story to life.'

And so we worked in silent concentration for the best part of two hours. I painted and repainted the gold borders using the quill and did the best I could to help Maya with the pictures. She took on the lizard, while I worked on a detailed picture of a bee, remembering the one that she'd shown me on the beach. I was focusing so hard on not spilling the ink that it gave me a headache. Maya's lizard was excellent. She definitely had a talent for drawing. By the end of the morning, we'd achieved a lot.

Finally, Teresa announced that it was time for lunch. She pulled from the oven a loaf of bread whose smell had filled the kitchen since morning. We ate it with a thick dollop of butter and bowls of soup.

Then she opened one of the windows in the main room and stuck her head out. She was listening for the dragon. Apart from the growl we'd heard yesterday and the alarming shaking of the ground, I had no idea what to expect of Yellow Eye and that was terrifying in itself. But Teresa seemed satisfied.

'You've both done a lot this morning. You need a break. Have an hour off now and get some air, but you must be careful. Perhaps you could take my horse, Apollo, to see Fikus, the farrier? His shoe has been loose for a few days now. But first ask Peter whether he needs him for any deliveries. His bakery is a two-minute walk down the hill to your left. The building with the red door.'

'It's no problem. We'll take him,' I said.

'Remember to stay together,' said Teresa. 'And stick to the main road. If you hear anything suspicious, what do you do?' she asked.

'Erm...'

'We go into the nearest building,' Maya said confidently, and I looked at her, impressed.

'Exactly. Shelter is a priority. As far as we're aware, Yellow Eye hasn't tried to destroy any buildings. Off you go and get Apollo.'

# 10

The minute we were out of the door, Maya grabbed my hand. 'We need to talk,' she said.

She pulled me into an alleyway off the main street where we were hidden from sight. Above our heads somebody had hung out their laundry, so the place was cold but fresh.

I leaned against the wall. Maya sat on an upturned bucket. I couldn't get used to this version of her, with her neat hair and pressed apron. But I was relieved to see the telltale signs of the personality I'd instantly liked. The shoelace on one of her boots was undone, both of her hair ribbons had come loose, and she was looking with wonder at everything around her, in exactly the same way she'd done that day on the beach.

'We're here. We're really here,' she said breathlessly, as if she'd truly realised the enormity of it for the first time.

'Yep.' I wasn't sure what else to say.

'Yesterday was awful. I was so scared. I don't think I've ever been so scared.'

'I know. I'm sorry, Maya. This is my fault. I – I somehow got us here and I need to find a way to…'

'Kon, the strangest thing happened last night.'

'The whole thing was surreal,' I agreed. 'Time travel, dragons, the books…'

'No, that's not what I meant. After you went upstairs, I couldn't sleep. Teresa made me a bed by the stove. She was finishing off something, and she was being really quiet, so that she wouldn't wake me. I pretended to sleep. Then there was a light knock on the door. I heard a woman's voice. She'd brought Teresa milk and apples, because she had some spare. She knew that we were staying with her. There was something about her voice that was so familiar. In the end, I couldn't help it and I turned around. She sounded exactly like my avó.'

'Your avó?'

Maya looked at the ground. Absentmindedly, she drew a circle in the dirt with a stick.

'I opened my eyes, and the two of them saw me. She reminded me so much of my avó. Of what she might look like now, I mean. And maybe I'm being ridiculous, but she smiled at me in a way that made me think she knew me – really knew who I was. Teresa introduced us, but it was almost as though there was no need.'

'Did she say anything else?'

'They were talking about the dragon and Teresa asked her whether she's scared of him. At first, I thought it was a silly question because obviously everyone is scared of the dragon. But this woman said she's not.'

'Why?'

'She said she sensed that there's someone in the town who knows how to approach him in the right way.'

'And who's that?'

'Us,' she said. 'I think it's us.'

'She said that?'

'No, no. I just think so. You know your dad said that for every person there's a corresponding character in a story? Well, I think we've found ours. And we've been put here to solve the problem of the dragon. We won't be able to get back to our world until we do.'

I was so relieved to hear her say that – well, not that we had a dragon to deal with, but because I'd been thinking the same. I slid down the wall I was leaning against, until I was sitting facing her.

'Maya, do you remember when I told you that the writing in the green book had disappeared?'

'Yeah. When we first arrived here.'

'Well, you'll never believe it, but a bit of it has come back. It's not much – just the opening few lines – I have a feeling that there will be more.'

'Maybe it'll reveal to us what we need to do?' she asked hopefully. 'We need to keep checking back to see what else has appeared in it.'

'That's what I was thinking too. In the meantime, let's gather as many facts as we can about the dragon and the city. We'd better begin by fetching Apollo,' I said, pulling her to her feet.

Work was in full flow at the bakery, even though it was already early afternoon. I could see three women and two men working at the back of the building behind the shop. One of them was rolling balls of dough into what looked like a giant pizza. Others were busy making different types of fillings. The shelves, which I guessed would have normally displayed cakes and pies, were completely empty and there were no customers. In fact, nobody noticed our arrival.

'Excuse me?' I called to the woman nearest to us. 'Do you know where Peter is?'

'Peter!' she bellowed, and he appeared suddenly through a side door, looking flustered.

'What is it?' I saw his tired face and a familiar-looking crease in the centre of his forehead. My heart leaped.

The woman beckoned us towards him.

'Oh, it's you two,' he said. 'It's chaotic here. I need to find more workers. There's no way we'll reach the food quota for today, let alone the rest of the week.'

'Does that mean that the dragon will starve?' asked Maya, concerned, and Peter raised his eyebrows in surprise at her question.

'It would be a while until he actually starved. But before that happens, he'll be furious that we haven't provided enough food and then what will he do? He's already made us fear for our lives every time we leave our houses. He's destroyed the king's most prized collection of books. I'm so glad that I was able to get your help in creating more,' he said, looking at me seriously.

'*You* were the one who sent for me?' I asked. 'But why…?'

He took a while to answer, looking at us in turn as if mulling over his answer.

'I've always been a great lover of books. I was lucky that my uncle was well-educated and taught me how to read. Isn't it incredible how books can be portals into different worlds?'

'Definitely,' I whispered.

'That's why I feel so strongly when they are destroyed. Anyway, I've known Father Stefan for years and I thought that you would be the right person for the job of restoration. Call it intuition,' he said, smiling at me. 'And it's clear that Maya has played a very important role too. How is the work going?'

'All right,' I said carefully. 'We understand exactly what needs doing. It's a bigger task than we thought it would be, but we're determined. We've taken a break so that we can get Apollo to the farrier. Did you need him this afternoon?'

'I was supposed to do that days ago. You would be doing me – and him – a huge favour. Here, take this.'

He took a leather purse from the pocket of his apron and handed me three coins. 'Thank you. I hope to see you this evening, if I manage to get the dragon's order done on time.'

As we left the bakery, a trumpet call sounded.

'It's on the hour every hour,' said Maya. 'It's a good way of telling the time without a phone or a watch.'

'As good as your sun method?' I asked, winking, and she smiled properly for the first time since we'd arrived.

'Almost.'

'So what do we know so far about Yellow Eye?' I asked as we walked.

'We know that he has an insatiable appetite and that he gets mad if he doesn't get fed,' she said.

'And he destroys property,' I added. 'It seems to be only small things at the moment. But it could be buildings next, and who knows what else.'

'Yesterday, the woman who came to speak to Teresa, who reminded me of my avó, said she thought that Yellow Eye had become more unpredictable. At first, he used to go out between one a.m. and four a.m. and wander around the town, looking for things to eat, even though there were huge piles of food put in front of his cave every morning at seven a.m. But now he leaves his cave more often. Yesterday was the second time he left during the day. Those were the growls we heard in the afternoon. He went all the way down to the riverbank, where the schoolhouse is. The kids were scared to come home after their lessons.'

'It looks like we've arrived at exactly the right time, doesn't it?' I said, feeling a sudden shiver of anticipation. 'And you know the best thing about all this? We know how the legend ends. We need to find Skuba, the farrier's apprentice.'

'But, Konrad, that ending is so violent. No animal deserves to be given something that will burn its insides so much that it drinks a river dry. And then explodes! The poor creature.'

'He's a beast.'

'Beast or no beast, I won't let them do that to him. We need another way. There *must* be another way.'

'They've already tried and nothing's worked.'

'I asked Teresa about it last night,' said Maya. 'It turns out they *actually* haven't done that much. They've increased food production to make sure that he's always fed. He's been here for nearly a month and the king is scared to do anything else, in case it angers Yellow Eye. Apparently the first week he arrived, the king ordered his men to shoot him with arrows. They had no effect – they bounced off his scaly skin. But the dragon was furious, and he picked up one of the marble pillars outside the castle entrance and threw it all the way down the hill. It caused serious damage to a couple of houses and injured a serving maid.'

'OK, let me think about this,' I said, as we reached the stables.

A tired-looking stable boy was tending a horse, brushing its mane. He had thick blond hair, with a fringe that he kept swiping away from his eyes with the back of his hand. When he stood up, we could see that he was pretty tall, but not much older than us.

'Good day,' he said, smiling. 'I'm Adam. I'm glad you came. Hardly a soul comes to the stables these days. I can't blame them, I suppose. People are scared to leave their houses. Are you bakery workers?'

'No, but we know Peter at the bakery. We're here to work with Teresa the scribe. We're creating new books to replace those ruined by the dragon.'

'He's even destroyed books?' asked Adam. 'Well, it's only a matter of time before the beast takes over the town. What's worse is that we're letting him do it.'

'Letting him, how?' I asked, surprised. 'Surely we don't have a choice?'

'We're feeding him. If you know Peter, you might have seen my older brothers, Igor and Tom. They've gone to work at the bakery today. Near enough everyone is making food for Yellow Eye. Fear is turning us mad. And still there's no plan from the king. Anyway, excuse my moaning. I've had nobody to talk to all day. How can I help you?'

'We're here for Apollo.'

'Ah, yeah. He needs a new shoe, doesn't he? Poor fellow. With all the madness, nobody's had a chance to see to him. Still, he's been fed so he'll be in good spirits. The dragon doesn't like the same food as horses, so at least they're in luck.'

We watched as he finished gently tending to Apollo, cleaning his ears and brushing his mane.

'What *does* Yellow Eye like to eat?' asked Maya.

'When he first came, the men saw him digging up slugs, snails and worms in huge quantities. When they ran out, he started raging from hunger. He devoured entire roast chickens. And when we had a shortage of those, pies and bread, which he seems to enjoy. Now all the bakeries have gone into overdrive. The only trouble is that they'll run out of wheat. But Yellow Eye turns his nose up at vegetables or fruit. So maybe he'll get scurvy sooner or later. Then our problem will be solved.'

He laughed, but it was an empty, hollow-sounding laugh, like Teresa's the other night. Everyone in Kraków felt they were walking on a knife's edge.

Out of the corner of my eye, I saw Maya stroking Apollo. I was worried that he might be scared or refuse to cooperate, but the minute he saw Maya, he rubbed his nose into her hair, as if he'd known her for ever. She went on stroking his head and waited for Adam to put on his bridle.

'He seems fond of you,' Adam said, as he watched Apollo raise his head to look straight at Maya. 'I haven't seen him this happy in days.'

Apollo didn't seem bothered by my presence at all. But with Maya, there was an instant bond.

We said goodbye to Adam. Maya took hold of the reins and together we led Apollo slowly down the hill. He was limping slightly, trying to avoid putting weight on his left front foot.

'You're a beautiful animal,' said Maya, stroking his ear as we walked. 'Don't worry, we'll get you sorted out in no time.'

'What breed do you think he is?' she asked me, but I was thinking how I could find out if Skuba worked with Fikus the farrier. Even if he didn't, I thought that Fikus might know him. Maya wouldn't be pleased. I would have to do it quietly.

It was easy to find the farriers because of the deafening noise coming from the building. There were men bringing horses in and out, the clanking sound of metal against metal, and apprentices shouting instructions. In all the chaos, I wasn't sure who to approach, but a young man tending to a horse near the entrance called, 'Can I help?'

'Yes, actually. We need somebody to put on a new shoe. It's the left front leg,' said Maya.

'Take him over to the boy finishing up with that mare, and he'll do it for you.'

As Maya led Apollo over, I leaned in towards the young man and taking advantage of the din, asked: 'Do you know if Skuba works here?'

'Skuba? Yeah, he's usually in. He's been off sick

this past week. Heard he's on the mend, though. He should be back within the week.'

'Great, thank you.' But we didn't have a week. I thought about asking if he knew where Skuba lived, when Maya reappeared.

'He said that it will take half an hour at most,' she said. 'Let's wait outside. It's too loud in here.'

Stepping into the street, I pulled Maya back as a cart nearly collided with us. I'd had an idea.

'Hey, Maya, so far, everyone has been leaving food outside Yellow Eye's cave, haven't they? But what if he woke up to a trail of delicious things? He'd follow it until he was full. We could make sure that the trail led far, far away, out of town.'

I remembered Dad telling me that there were forests everywhere around medieval Kraków. Surely it would be possible to lead the dragon into the depths of one and then he'd lose his way. He'd have to live off the land and make a home for himself there.

'It could work...' she said thoughtfully. 'But there are a few problems. How would we get enough food? And how would we transport it out of the town? In our world, we'd use a massive van for something like that, wouldn't we?'

'We know where the food is. The townspeople leave it outside the cave around seven every morning before the dragon wakes up. Let's say that we get there half an hour earlier. Adam could help us get a cart. We'd use Apollo and maybe another horse to pull the cart out of town and we'd drop the food off the back as we went. We'd have to time it perfectly so that Yellow Eye didn't have a chance to catch up with us.'

'Wouldn't somebody try to stop us if they saw that we were taking the food?'

'That's the thing. They're all so petrified of the dragon I bet there would be nobody around. Why don't we go to the castle early tomorrow morning to assess the situation? There's no harm in testing the theory.'

'I don't know...'

'He's ready!' called a voice from indoors and Maya went to fetch Apollo.

As we walked back up the hill, I saw the worry on her face. 'Why don't *I* go?' I said. 'One of us should stay in the house in case Teresa wakes up. She's the kind of person who would raise the alarm and have the whole town looking for us in no time. There's a ledge outside my bedroom window. I could easily use it to lower myself down.'

'That sounds pretty dangerous, especially at night.'

'The ceilings are so low here that I could make it to the ground easily. I'll go at the crack of dawn, when there's already some light.'

'You might have to go earlier than that if you want to make it before he wakes up. I've seen Teresa light a candle using flint and steel. I reckon I could do it. I'll get up with you and have it ready for when you leave. It won't be much, but it might help guide you before it gets light. But, Kon…?'

'Yeah?'

'Be careful,' she said, her voice shaking. 'Don't get too close. This is a dragon we're talking about.'

11

I was scared that I wouldn't wake up. I could really have done with my watch with its inbuilt alarm. Maya had told me that the trumpet call was on the hour, every hour, even through the night. Apparently between nine in the evening and seven in the morning it wasn't quite so loud, and it certainly hadn't woken me yet.

I pulled the green book out and sat in bed, poring over it. The candlelight cast dancing shadows over the walls of my attic room as I stroked the cover, recalling the legends that Dad had told me. They still seemed so magical and far-fetched, yet here I was. For ages, I didn't dare open the book, worrying that nothing would have changed and that there would only be blank pages staring back at me.

Eventually, I took a deep breath, closed my eyes and whispered, 'Give us another clue.'

On the first page, I immediately saw that there was more text and the beautiful embellished picture of the dragon which I remembered so well. He was drawn in vivid reds and golds. He was standing by the entrance to his cave, next to a cartload of food. I wasn't sure whether my memory was deceiving me, but I felt that there was something slightly different about him. I parked this niggling thought and decided to return to it later. The story stopped just before the moment in which Skuba was due to enter the scene, but there wasn't anything unusual about it.

Eventually, I shut the book and watched the candle burn out, still thinking about the picture of the dragon. When I felt myself growing tired, I tried to count the seconds and minutes until the trumpeter made his call.

But I must have fallen asleep, because I woke to the sound of the trumpet. It was dark outside and I guessed that it must be four o'clock, the time I'd agreed to meet Maya by the front door. It was as if my brain had somehow known when to rouse me.

I grabbed the fleece overcoat Teresa had given me, and my shoes, and quietly opened the window, listening for Teresa's steady snores. Somewhere below me the lock creaked. Maya. She appeared holding two candles, both of which cast surprisingly bright flames. She put one on the lower window sill and held the other aloft, putting her finger to her lips.

I climbed on to the window ledge and got into a crouching position. The hours spent with Dad scaling rocks around the coast had come in useful at last. I lowered myself on to the ledge below where Maya's candle stood and jumped on to the cobbles. I was surprised at how easy it was.

'Good luck,' said Maya, pulling me into a hug. 'I'll be listening out for you when you get back.'

'I won't take any risks,' I promised, as I set off down the street.

It was the middle of spring, but I felt chilled to the bone. The sky had been full of stars, and now they were dissolving in the morning light. I remembered Dad telling me once that it was as though a giant had been making a cake and had sprinkled his celestial table with a smattering of silver flour.

The street was silent but a rustle of something in the trees beyond made me turn nervously. There was nobody there. It must have been a bird or a rabbit.

I climbed the hill using the backstreets which were completely dark, despite dawn being not far off. I was guided by Maya's candle, and the occasional brightly lit window. I imagined that inside they were either making food for Yellow Eye, or maybe they couldn't sleep because they were so scared.

I hadn't heard him that night, but that didn't mean he hadn't roamed the town. Over supper, Teresa had told us that earlier in the week, she'd twice sat bolt upright in bed, certain he was only a few strides from her window. She'd thought she could hear his raspy breathing and another agitated sound – somewhere between a moan and a shriek. I shuddered to think I would soon hear it with my own ears.

As I neared the turning that led to the lower gates, I froze. There were voices nearby. I edged close to a building so I wouldn't be visible and saw a crowd milling, illuminated by huge, lit torches.

A vast silhouette of the castle loomed above me shrouded in grey dawn. It almost looked as if it had been carved into the rockface. The last thing I saw as I emerged from the gloom was the opening of a cave.

Men in uniforms, with gold buttons glinting in the torchlight, busily unloaded the carts. The only noise, apart from their subdued conversation, was the occasional frightened neighing of horses. Everyone worked quickly and methodically. I guessed that they'd gone through the same process many times.

'Bring them closer. Put the pies in front of the tree, by the cave entrance,' said a tall man, who seemed to be managing the operation. 'He needs to smell them.'

'He'll be able to smell them. Don't make me go in there,' a younger voice pleaded. 'I have a wife and a baby. I promised I would return in one piece.'

'We all have reasons for wanting to stay alive,' snapped the leader. 'Do as I say, and we'll be able to get out of here faster.'

The unloading continued. I edged closer and counted about thirty people, mainly soldiers.

The cave was swathed in a darkness inkier than the surrounding night. In the dim light of the soldiers' lanterns, I saw a dense, rising mist. And that was when the smell hit me with full force, making my head reel. It was a mix of sulphur and earth and a rocky dampness that reminded me suddenly and painfully of home. Cold seeped through me, making my bones shudder.

The minute the soldiers had unloaded everything, they retreated and all that was left was a deafening silence, disturbed only by a regular rasp from the cave. It was the dragon breathing. He was there in the darkness, sleeping as I watched and waited.

I tried to time the minutes in my head, but I soon lost count. The sun began to rise. Above the row of houses, a faint orange glow spread across the sky and then a touch of pink, as if the sky was blushing. In front of me, the castle revealed itself – a mass of turrets, towers, curtain walls and a portcullis. In the morning mist, it was difficult to see where the rock ended and the building began. The gates gleamed gold and the windows shone as the first rays of sunlight pierced the mist.

I wondered what the king and his family must feel, sleeping, eating and going about their days directly above the dragon's cave. I'd been puzzled that the king hadn't ordered his family to be evacuated while Yellow Eye was sleeping. But Teresa had told me a lot of it was pride. 'Think about it, if the king left the castle, what message would that send to the townsfolk? Everybody would run. By holding down the fort, he's showing everyone that we're in this together.'

I felt the dragon's presence and I thought suddenly about the creature in the green book. But in my mind's eye he grew larger and more terrifying than any picture I'd ever seen. I could sense his rage.

I heard movement in the houses around me, and the faces of two children appeared in a lower window, looking towards the castle. But the streets remained deserted.

Nobody had told me what actually happened when the dragon woke, probably because they didn't know. I was aware of the danger that I was in, yet my curiosity got the better of me. I needed to see this beast that Dad had painted so brilliantly in my head.

After the trumpet call sounded for seven o'clock, I heard it. A high-pitched shriek, the scraping of claws against rock. My hands flew to my ears to stop the deafening, terrible sound. The ground shook and I saw soldiers dispersing as panic whipped through the town.

I was no more than ten metres from the entrance to Yellow Eye's cave. If he couldn't see me, he would definitely be able to smell me from here, just as I could smell his foul breath.

But even if I wanted to run, I couldn't. My legs were glued to the ground. I was paralysed by fear ... and excitement. I was finally about to meet the dragon from my favourite legend. From Dad's legend. And then I saw him. Eyes gleaming yellow, fiery scales glistening, sparks shooting dangerously from his mouth. He was impossibly tall, powerful and unquestionably a dragon.

I heard Dad's voice in my ear: 'Megalosaurus? Notice the long hind limbs and small fore limbs. Although ... he's more active in the day rather than at night. So perhaps we're not on the right track.'

It immediately calmed my rattling heart. I forced myself to imagine that I was looking at a lifelike exhibit at the Natural History Museum.

'But he's living in the wrong historical period, Dad,' I responded. 'And notice the colour – an orangey-red hue. Surely this can't be a dinosaur?'

'Not everything is quite as you expect, though, is it?'

The dragon's head was small in comparison to the rest of his body, but his jaws and teeth were huge. They could easily crush a human with a single bite. His neck was thick and muscular, and his glistening body was larger and more imposing than anything I'd ever imagined. Then there was a strange rustling sound and something happened which made me certain that this wasn't a Megalosaurus. Because the creature stood up, causing the ground to shake, and it gradually unfolded a pair of enormous wings. They were webbed and semi-translucent and clearly strong enough to allow him to fly.

He stretched them and then folded them back in as he sniffed the air outside his cave. His tail was so thick and long that I'd mistaken it for the rockface, not realising it was attached to him.

'Look at the claws, Kon,' Dad's voice said quietly, and I stared at the three prongs, the familiar shape imprinted on my memory.

The dragon lashed his tail, causing sparks to fly where it grazed the ground, and then proceeded to use his claws to carelessly shovel the food laid in front of him into his giant mouth.

I stared as mountains of pies, loaves of bread and other delicacies disappeared down his throat in an instant.

The oddest thing was that the dragon seemed not to enjoy his food. It was as though he'd come to expect it. He didn't seem any more satisfied by the time that he'd devoured the very last morsel.

I watched as he spat out bones and brushed leftover debris into the bushes to clear his path.

There was a moment when the tip of his tail was so close to me that it brushed my leg. I was certain he would sense my presence and I was about to break into a run, when he turned away to the left-hand side of the cave, up the cobbled path and past the entrance of the castle.

I breathed out, wondering where he was going, and remembered Teresa telling me about the insatiable thirst that usually followed his hunger.

'He goes to the riverbank to drink,' she'd told us. 'Fishermen have seen him drinking an immense amount.'

I thought of the end of the legend that Dad had read to me so many times. But Maya wouldn't let me go ahead with this version of events. In fact, she was determined that no harm would come to the dragon. So we would have to try the other method.

How would Yellow Eye react if he was made to work for his food? If he was forced to follow a trail all the way beyond the outskirts of the town? We were about to find out.

## 12

Maya threw me a relieved look when I returned and motioned that I climb back up to my bedroom. In the background, I glimpsed Teresa. As Maya distracted her, I checked to see I wasn't being watched, then swung myself on to the first ledge and then the second. I barely made it, because moments later, Teresa was calling me for breakfast.

Maya and I were exhausted. We spent the entire morning diligently copying out our first book. I was certain that we'd make mistakes, but the process seemed to go surprisingly smoothly and by lunchtime, we more or less had the first draft completed. I flicked through the pages, which rustled with stories, and I suddenly felt a glimmer of pride. When it was bound, this would become much like the book of legends I used to read with Dad.

'I'm pleased with this,' said Teresa, glancing over our shoulders at the intricate illustrations. 'Just think – someone in the future will read this one day and it will stir wonder within them. They'll enter an entirely new universe, thanks to you. That's the magic of making books.'

Her comment made me think of the green book and I disappeared upstairs, saying I needed to get something. I opened it, certain that by now a new clue must have appeared. But I was disappointed to find nothing had changed. The story was stuck in exactly the same place as before.

A few minutes later, when we managed to get outside, I was desperate to figure out with Maya what was happening with it. Maybe the lack of new words was a clue in itself?

But as we headed into our alleyway, she wanted to know everything about the dragon, so I described what I'd seen in detail.

'I still can't believe you got so close to him! If I'd

known you'd do that, I would have stopped you going,' she said, half-freaked-out, half-impressed.

'But it was worth it, wasn't it? We know it's possible now. And we know exactly what time and where they unload the carts of food, and that there's nobody around after they go. It's practically a perfect situation for putting our plan into action!'

'There's no way we'll be able to do it alone,' she said. 'We need to speak to Adam. Do you reckon he'll help? He might be too scared, or not want to take the risk.'

'There's only one way to find out. But, Maya, the story's stuck. The main part of it, which talks about Skuba the farrier appearing on the scene, that hasn't returned to the page. Do you think it's because we haven't managed to speak to him yet?'

'But he's sick,' said Maya. 'So we need to find a different way.' She threw me such a determined look that I didn't want to argue with her.

Luckily, Adam was alone with the horses when we went back on the pretext of visiting Apollo. I wondered whether Adam went entire days without seeing another human being.

His eyes widened as I began to tell him my plan.

'It's not guaranteed,' I added. 'But what alternative do we have? Wait until there's no food left, and we starve?'

He didn't say anything for some time and then let out a sudden laugh.

'Do you think I'm a fool for thinking it could work?' I asked.

He wiped his blond fringe off his face and shook his head. 'The opposite. I'm laughing at why nobody has thought of this before. All our efforts have been on killing the dragon and when that didn't work, on placating him, but nobody's considered trying to lead him away. It's risky and it might not work, but it's worth a try.'

'Can you help us? We'd need a cart and another horse to help Apollo pull it.'

'I can give you Electra,' he said, pointing to a white, beautifully groomed mare. 'She's easygoing and obedient. She'll do what you ask and she's well-acquainted with Apollo.'

'And will you come with us?' asked Maya. 'We could use some help.'

'I want to be part of this,' he said. 'I know a farmer who will lend us a cart. So we would take the empty cart to the castle, and load it up with the food left there? But what if someone sees us and thinks we're stealing?'

'They won't. No one wants to be there when the dragon wakes up,' I reassured him. 'And even if someone does see us, they wouldn't dare raise an alarm. It would be too dangerous.'

'Are Apollo and Electra fast?' asked Maya. 'What if the dragon chases us and we don't manage to escape?'

'You make a fair point. Timing is of great importance.'

'How do you mean?'

'We'll need to make sure that we leave before the dragon wakes up, so that we can maximise the distance between us. If Apollo and Electra catch a glimpse of him, we could be in trouble. They've heard the noises he makes and let's just say they didn't like them.'

I'd been feeling pretty confident until he'd said that. Maya stroked Apollo's neck and he whickered, as if he knew that we were talking about him.

'Maybe we should wait a while,' she said. 'We can see how the situation develops and learn more about Yellow Eye's behaviour. We only have one chance, and we don't want it to end in disaster.'

Adam shook his head. 'No. We need to act as quickly as possible. Kraków is running out of food. It's now or never.'

He was right, of course. The green book swam back into my mind. What if we were doing things wrong and the rest of the story never appeared? Would we be stuck here for ever? The thought made me feel sick.

'The cart can be ready tonight,' Adam promised. 'My friend has no use for it, as he won't be taking his goods to the market. We'll need more hands to help load the food, otherwise we won't get it on to the cart in time. I'll ask my brothers. They'll agree if they're not working the night shift at the bakery.'

'I'm really not sure,' said Maya, and I could see her nervously picking the skin around her fingernails.

At that moment a tremor shot through my body and the ground beneath our feet began to shake. I grabbed hold of Maya and we clutched each other tight.

Clumps of straw from the roof of the stable fell around us, the horses whinnied, and Apollo reared as if readying for battle. In the distance, panicked commands were shouted, interspersed with that strange and awful roar, partway between a moan and a shriek, louder and more forceful than any noise I'd heard a living creature make. Maya covered her ears in pain, as a jolt of terror ran through me.

Adam grabbed Apollo and a grey mare to his left, trying to calm them. He whispered gently in their ears and looked them straight in the eye, reassuring them that everything was going to be OK. I couldn't believe how soothing he could be when the world around him was literally shaking.

When he moved on to the next pair of horses, Maya ran to Apollo and wrapped her arms around his neck. Somehow, between the three of us, we managed to prevent the horses from freaking out and galloping off.

The shaking gradually subsided and the next shriek, when it came, seemed much further away.

'He's gone to the north of the town,' said Adam, listening. 'Now's your chance to travel home.'

'Can you meet us here?' I asked. 'Maybe at four in the morning? That should give us enough time.'

'I'll be here,' he said firmly.

As we left the stables, a bitter tang of smoke swirled above us, and I could taste the fear in the air. Children's faces were pressed to the windows, parents trying to usher them further inside. Men and women flattened themselves against buildings, scared they might encounter the dragon. There was shouting and suddenly a scream cut through the air.

Maya and I exchanged a look. We knew something terrible had happened.

'This is the end!' an old man wailed.

We saw an overturned cart in the middle of the street, fruit spilled in all directions, most of it trampled to pulp. It was obvious what had happened.

Before I could stop her, Maya started to pick up whatever fruit could be salvaged and put it into the few unbroken baskets.

Without thinking, I grabbed some apples and did the same, piling anything that could be saved next to the old man.

'Oh, thank you,' he said. 'Never in my seventy-five years have I seen anything like that. Never,' he kept saying over and over. 'Beast is not even the right word to describe it. The savage! The brute! He used only to come out at night, but now leaves his cave any time of day. There's no way that we will ever be able to get rid of him. I've lived a long and a good life. But what about the children? What about you?'

Luckily, his wife appeared and took him indoors, and we followed with our pitiful-looking baskets.

'Take one,' she said. 'It's the least you deserve for your help.'

We thanked them, but refused, and ran back to Teresa's.

She hugged us tightly as we burst through the door.

'Thank goodness you're safe. I should have known not to let the two of you out. The dragon is becoming more and more unpredictable.'

'It sounded bad,' I told her. 'Something's happened. Something worse than usual.'

'I suppose we'll learn what soon enough,' she said resignedly. 'The main thing is that you're here.'

For a while, we stood by the windows to see whether there would be any further commotion, but it had died down. Teresa prepared dumplings for dinner and we tried to settle back into copying scripts, even though our thoughts were elsewhere.

I heard the scream over and over in my mind. Now that I'd seen Yellow Eye in the flesh, my imagination was more vivid than ever. I visualised him lifting animals and even people in his mighty claws and hurling them the length of a street or field. I saw houses toppled, buildings destroyed and people running for their lives.

The dragon had stepped from the pages of the legend and was as terrifying as the story foretold. I couldn't help thinking of that paragraph of the legend which I knew so well...

*...He was the fear of every inhabitant of the town, as they closed their shutters tight, barricaded their doors with sacks of flour, and burned incense, hoping that he would stay away. He didn't, of course.*

Peter appeared in our doorway just before dinner and sat at the end of the table, exhausted. His blue eyes were red-rimmed with tiredness and his fingers were blistered.

'He destroyed Sikora's farm,' he said. 'Trampled it to the ground. The building is gone. He's eaten all their supplies, and even destroyed their fruit trees. They have nothing left.'

'But why did he go there in particular?' I asked. 'Was it random?'

'That's the strangest thing. Nobody knows,' Peter admitted. 'He's never targeted a place like that before. Apparently Mr Sikora's daughter was in the outhouse, singing her baby to sleep. The little boy prefers the coolness of that building. They survived because of that. If they had been in the main house, they would have died.'

'Was there *anyone* in the main house?' asked Maya.

'Luckily not. The others were out working in the field. They managed to get away in time. Their neighbours have taken them in for now and offered them a place to sleep.'

As we finished our dinner, I could see Teresa getting more and more nervous. She'd barely touched the stew she'd slaved over last night.

'What is it?' I asked. 'Are you worried about what happened at the farm?'

'I have to go out, Kon. I promised to deliver the first two completed books to the king's country estate,' she said, pointing to a small, neatly wrapped parcel on the table.

'You mean yours and the one that we completed?' I couldn't believe that our book was actually going to be seen by the king. Teresa had bound it now, and when I saw her remove it from its leather pouch, a gasp of disbelief escaped my mouth. Because the cover looked like an almost exact replica of the green book that I had upstairs. Although this one, of course, had the full title on it: *The Book of Ancient Legends*, and I knew for certain that our legend wasn't there. It clearly hadn't been written yet!

'Don't look at me like that,' Teresa said. 'I know I'm taking a risk, but I pride myself on keeping my word. It's a fair distance from the castle and the king thinks that they'll be safe there. He wants to make sure that these two copies at least are saved, in case there's any further damage.'

'I'll go,' said Peter straight away.

'No.' I could hear the determination in her voice. 'I said I'd go, so I will. You stay here with Maya and Konrad. I won't be long.'

She was out of the door before any of us could utter another word. For a few moments we sat in silence. My heart missed a beat, as I thought about the two different versions of the book. What did it mean?

I felt an arm round my back, squeezing my shoulder reassuringly. The gesture was familiar, and I heard Peter say, 'It's going to be all right, you know.' My anxiety began to lift, like a cloud of steam dispersing.

'Let me make the two of you something to drink.'

So I helped to prepare Maya's bed, as Peter made us hot coriander water and told us stories from his childhood. We tried our best not to think about the danger that Teresa might be in. For a blissful hour it was as though the dragon had never existed.

We learned that Peter's uncle had been one of the professors at the famous Kraków Academy. I gathered that it was a super-special school and very few kids attended – mostly those from rich families who knew the king.

'When I was little, I used to meet my uncle at the Cloth Hall after he'd finished lectures,' he said. 'We would listen to the trumpet call from the tower because it would usually be exactly four o'clock. The timing has always been precise, and we had a great view of the trumpeter, because the halls were directly opposite.'

'Why is it such an odd sound?' I asked. 'The tune seems to stop quite abruptly.'

'You don't know this story, Kon?' he asked, looking at me closely. 'It's from when the Mongol army from East Asia attacked Kraków around one hundred years ago. Their plan was to storm the town. Luckily, a watchman at the top of St Mary's Basilica sounded the alarm and the gates to the town were closed before the enemy army could invade.'

'…And the watchman was shot in the throat by one of the enemy soldiers, so he couldn't complete the anthem,' I finished breathlessly. I remembered Dad explaining this story to me one night when we'd been reading the book of legends.

'So they play it in his honour?' asked Maya. 'And stop at the exact point he stopped playing that day?'

'That's right,' said Peter. 'On the hour, every hour. It's funny how we all manage to sleep through it. I suppose we're used to it by now. Anyway, going back to what I was saying about my uncle. After we'd listened to the trumpet call, he would buy me dumplings from the stalls in the Cloth Hall. They were even tastier than Teresa's, but don't tell her that. I think the women who ran the stalls had some sort of special recipe. They were very peculiar. Some called them soothsayers. Their recipes were divine,' he said, closing his eyes. 'Oh, what I wouldn't give for a few of those dumplings.'

'Where are those women now?' asked Maya.

'Well, I can tell you where they *were*. If they weren't running their stalls, we would find them in the cellars beneath the Cloth Hall. I don't think that was their home, but they always seemed to be there, lurking in the dark. My friend Alfred's father was a leather merchant, and when we arrived home after school, he would send us to the cellars to get more of his wares. At first, we had the fright of our lives when we saw those women in the shadows. They never did anything particularly scary, but they spoke in a way that made you feel as though they knew everything about you. There was one in particular, called Galatea, who I became good friends with. She helped me to ... understand some things which I couldn't get my head around. I think perhaps you've had the pleasure of meeting her?' he asked, glancing over at Maya.

'The woman who came here the other day?' asked Maya. 'She had long, grey hair tied up in a plait and I thought she looked a lot like...'

'That's her,' said Peter.

'What things did she help you understand?' I asked. I felt an urge to know. But at that moment,

Teresa appeared in the doorway, triumphant. In the dim light of her oil lamp, I could see sweat glistening on her face.

'I did it,' she announced. 'I managed to get a ride there on a delivery cart and the man was kind enough to wait and bring me home. You wouldn't believe how glad I am to be back.'

I was so relieved and happy when I lay down in bed later. It seemed unbelievable that in just a few hours we'd be getting up to take on the biggest creature that any of us had ever seen. Maya had somehow managed to fall asleep even before I went upstairs. I was envious of her ability to doze off despite the drama. For me, sleep didn't come. Peter's comment about Galatea played on my mind, like a cryptic element of another, fresh puzzle, which I'd need to examine when the time was right.

13

I opened my eyes to find Maya shaking me.

'It's time,' she said. 'I just heard the trumpet call.' Her teeth were chattering even though the room was warm. 'Teresa is sound asleep. I accidentally scraped a chair, but she didn't wake. Oh, Kon, do you really think we should be doing this?' she whispered.

'Yes,' I said, pulling myself up. 'It's now or never.' I hoped that the more I repeated the phrase, the more confident I'd feel. It wasn't really working so far.

I dressed and we climbed down the ladder. I felt awful for not telling Teresa what we were up to, especially as we'd promised that we wouldn't leave the house without her until it was safe. But I knew that she wouldn't support our plan, and it would only cause problems.

The night was colder than it had been yesterday. Outside, we listened for any sign of danger. All was quiet. It was so silent that when an owl hooted, Maya jumped and stumbled into me.

'We're OK,' I said, squeezing her hand. 'We need to stick together. Everyone will be doubly cautious after what happened earlier. It's good news for us. Word will have spread about the farm, and the men dealing with the food delivery will scarper even more quickly than yesterday.'

'I hope Adam's there,' she said nervously.

But we needn't have worried, because he was waiting for us outside the gates to the stable with his brothers.

In the light of the oil lamp one of his brothers was holding, I saw he was finishing harnessing the horses. Everything was set for our journey.

'Good morrow, I'm Igor, and this is Tom,' said the boy holding the lamp. He was tall and muscular, and looked about sixteen.

Tom was younger and thinner, with an eager

glimmer in his eye. 'You have great courage,' he said. 'I'm rooting for you.'

'We'll need to park the cart a fair distance away so that they don't see us. We can always pull up closer to the castle gates when the coast is clear,' Adam instructed. 'Jump in!'

Maya hesitated, and then she hitched up her skirt and stepped on to the ledge. She swung her leg over and sat in the back of the cart. I followed quickly, along with Igor and Tom.

Adam sat in the driver's seat and before any of us could change our minds, we were off.

Everything happened so quickly that it was barely half-past four.

'We're too early,' I said.

'Don't worry,' said Adam. 'Better early than late. It will give us a chance to get the measure of things. We'll see the food and work out how to pack it on to the cart.'

'Good thinking.'

I noticed that he was taking us the long way around the hill, which meant we were approaching the dragon's lair from the back.

'It's so they don't hear Apollo and Electra,' he said, as if guessing my thoughts. 'I'll stop them now and we'll go on foot from here. If we follow this alleyway, it will give us a perfect view of the dragon's cave from the left.'

Maya had closed her eyes and was clutching my wrist so tightly that her nails were making small, painful indentations.

'No matter what happens, it's important that you don't move,' Adam said, looking into the horses' eyes. 'You're helping us on a very special mission.'

Apollo whickered softly, as if to show that he understood.

'Will you come with us?' I asked Igor and Tom.

'We will help you load the cart, but after that, we must make haste. Our shift at the bakery starts in an hour. Besides, we didn't want to—'

'What?'

'It's our mother,' said Tom, staring at the ground. In the pale light of his oil lamp, I could see that his face wore an awkward expression. 'With our father gone, we can't afford for all three of us to— The risk is too great,' he managed eventually. 'You understand?'

Next to me Maya shifted, as the meaning of his words sank in. I wanted to protest that it was a risk worth taking, but Adam turned to us, his finger to his lips.

'I can hear the soldiers' horses,' he said. 'Let's go.'

We sneaked down the alley way to see what was going on. Adam had been right – it provided a far better view than the spot I'd chosen the previous night. When the silhouette of the castle came into sight, Maya gasped and positioned herself behind me.

'It's huge!' she whispered frantically. 'How enormous is he?'

'He's huge,' I whispered. 'But let's stay together. We can do this.'

I noticed the familiar odour coming from the cave and tried not to gag. A group of soldiers was unloading three carts in front of the cave. There were far fewer of them than yesterday and they were working in a much more panicked and haphazard way, as if they wanted to get the job over and done with as quickly as possible.

It could be that not all the food had arrived, but I got the sense that there was less of it. Perhaps we'd already reached the point in which Kraków had run out of supplies. I didn't dare think what would happen tomorrow and the day after that if we weren't successful.

I heard one of the soldiers call out, 'Lay down the two hay bales. Perhaps he'll eat them. It's worth a try!'

'He won't eat them, I tell you. And it's good hay. We need it for the livestock!'

There was further arguing, and eventually four frightened soldiers pulled the bales from the third cart and left them in front of the cave.

And then, before there were any further demands, the horses sprang into action and the clatter of hooves could be heard departing down the street. In the quiet of the night, the echo resounded long after they'd disappeared.

'That's it?' asked Maya. 'And there's nobody even guarding the cave?'

'No. Nobody dares,' said Adam. 'Yellow Eye's unpredictable. Before, they could at least count on him having a routine. Now everything's changed. As you know, instead of settling down to sleep, he was trampling a farm in the north of the town. He seems to be getting angrier. Nobody wants to risk their lives standing guard outside his cave. It's a death wish.'

'Well, it's a good thing for us, isn't it?' I whispered. 'It means that we won't be spotted.'

Tom and Igor fetched the horses and pulled them up behind the palace gates. We got to work loading the goods on to our cart. Adam instructed us to put all the heavy, solid food at the bottom, so we lined the base with roast chickens, cooked legs of lamb and joints of beef. The smell was delicious, and if it wasn't for the panic, I would have had trouble resisting the urge to tuck in. Next came the pies of various sizes and at the top, dumplings, loaves of bread and cakes.

Maya kept glancing in the direction of the cave. I was certain that at any moment the dragon would wake or someone in the surrounding houses would see us and raise the alarm. Maybe Adam hadn't been right. Maybe the police would come running and arrest us. I guessed that they must have some form of a police force here. Or perhaps punishments of this kind were given out by the soldiers? Worrying possibilities built in my head.

The cart was heaving and still there was food on the ground.

'We'll have to leave it. The poor horses won't be able to pull any more,' said Adam. 'They'll struggle as it is.'

'Let's go,' said Maya, wiping sweat off her forehead. She was so nervous that her hands had been shaking as she loaded the cart. 'The sun's beginning to rise. Yellow Eye's going to be up any minute.'

Tom and Igor bade us goodbye, and Adam flicked the reins to get the horses moving. I was scared that we'd loaded the cart too high and Apollo and Electra wouldn't be able to pull it, but they set off at a steady trot through the cobbled streets.

'Come and stand with me at the back of the cart,' I called to Maya. 'We need to leave the trail. Start with the light stuff on top. Drop the loaves of bread at regular intervals. Let's count to five between each drop.'

So I did the counting, and we took it in turns

to drop food off the cart. The rhythm of the task, and seeing the distance between us and Yellow Eye increase, made us less nervous.

I realised that we hadn't discussed with Adam where we were going, but he seemed to have a plan. Instead of heading down the hill, he instructed the horses to go in the direction of the river, where I'd last seen the dragon drink.

In the silence of the early morning, the horses' hooves and the squeaking of the cart's wheels caused an absolute racket, and I was worried that we might wake the king and the rest of the royal household. I braced myself and began to think up excuses. But we drove on uninterrupted.

Had I imagined it or were the horses speeding up, as their load got lighter? The rising sun reflected in the river like an orb, and by the time we were on the other side, it was practically light.

The houses were different on this bank – more widely spaced apart. We were surrounded by farmland and I wondered whether the farm that Yellow Eye had destroyed yesterday was nestled somewhere among these fields.

'Should we slow down a bit?' Maya asked, noticing the rapid rate at which the food was disappearing. We'd already got rid of almost all the pastries. We agreed to count to ten between each throw, as Adam quickened the horses' pace.

We rode through dusty lanes between fields of wheat and barley. I breathed a sigh of relief when I saw the edge of the forest – just a strip on the horizon but becoming clearer and more defined as we drew nearer. At last we had our goal in sight. If we managed to hide among the dense trees, we would have almost succeeded. We would be safe, and have a real chance of losing Yellow Eye.

Then, as my fear was turning into welcome relief, Maya squeezed my hand tightly. 'He's coming.'

I stopped throwing and followed the direction she was pointing. He was coming and he moved at quite a pace. Each stride he took was easily four or five lengths of Apollo's body, his long tail swinging powerfully behind him.

'The food is disappearing as if it's a snack to him,' said Maya, both horrified and amazed. 'It looks as if he doesn't even chew.'

'True, but he has to bend to pick it up and that's slowing him down because his fore legs are so short.' It clearly made the dragon frustrated and the high-pitched shriek pierced the air. A burst of flames shot from his nostrils.

'We have to pick up the pace!' I shouted to Adam. 'He's gaining on us!'

I shuffled to the front of the cart.

'We're going as fast as we can!' he said. 'It's quite a load to pull for the two of them. It would be wrong to push them hard now, they might give up on us entirely.' He was trying to sound calm, but I heard the concern in his voice.

We entered the forest and were met with a quiet coolness. The tightly packed trees drowned the dragon's shrieks and it almost felt as though we'd crossed the border from one world into another. I noticed how untouched our surroundings were. There didn't even seem to be a proper path through the trees, just a sandy bank along the edge of a river, which the horses trotted across.

'Do you know where you're going?' I asked Adam.

'Yes. I've been here before.'

'We're down to two pies and twelve roast chickens!' Maya called.

'Right. We need to spread them out and make them last. Fifteen seconds between each throw. It doesn't matter so much now, because he can see us.'

Adam diverted the horses from the river, and we wove through the trees, eventually reaching a clearing, where rays of sunlight pooled invitingly. In a different time and situation, this would have made the most perfect picnic spot.

But Adam didn't stop, although the horses were flagging. We dropped the last two pies off the cart, and I let him know that we were done. Then he drew the horses to a halt so that we could listen out for Yellow Eye. Nothing. A gentle breeze ruffled the leaves. Somewhere overhead birds sang. Apollo snorted softly. Otherwise, all was still. But somewhere deep within me, I knew that Yellow Eye was closer than ever.

'Did we lose him?' Maya whispered hopefully.

'Shhh. It's too early to —'

And then a shriek rang out, which terrified me to the core. He was in the forest.

'We need to lose him,' I whispered frantically to Adam, aware of the dragon's huge strides and our tired horses. What if they suddenly gave up? Or worse still, what if they saw the dragon moving through the trees and bolted?

Maya jumped out of the cart and pulled something from her pocket. Carrots. She fed them quickly to Apollo and Electra, stroking them behind their ears.

'Thank you,' I heard her say. 'Do you think you could take us a little further? It's important.'

Adam mobilised the horses and they began to move in a slow, but steady, trot.

We were deep in the forest now. I worried that we'd be so far in, we'd have no idea how to get back. Adam seemed in control. We would advance for a couple of minutes and then stop to listen. I told myself that the dragon's shriek was further away. The last two times we'd stopped there'd been no sound at all, only our ragged breathing and the wind stirring the trees.

I began to relax and talk to Maya about what we would tell Teresa, who would be beside herself with worry about us.

Just then, a piercing scream shot through the air so loudly that I fell to my knees with my hands over my ears. The horses startled at the sound and the cart jerked, almost falling on to its side. I became aware of an immense shape looming over me. Yellow Eye. He was so close that his hot breath fanned my face. His wings extended to their fullest reach, impossibly wide. Next to me, Maya screamed. The dragon lowered his head so that it was level with mine and sniffed. Panic rose in my throat. This was it. This was the end of us.

Yellow Eye reached forward with a golden claw and I shut my eyes. Time dragged endlessly. Then Dad's voice came to me, as if through a haze of memory. It carried on the wind and it sounded like Dad, but like somebody else too.

'Remember, Kon, intrepid explorers never let fear overwhelm them,' he said. 'Stare that fear in the face. See it for what it really is. I'm with you. Surely you know that by now. You don't have to be afraid.'

And to my surprise, I found that I wasn't.

'Stop!' I shouted. 'Don't come any closer! We've given you all the food we have. You must leave this town now. We have nothing more to give you!'

A growl rose from within Yellow Eye's chest, sending tremors through the forest. His back legs gouged the ground as if he was getting ready to attack and his tail cut the air.

I dared myself to stare into his face and I saw that he was listening. He froze, mid-movement, trying to read me.

I pointed blindly to my right.

'Go!' I screamed.

He blinked and sank back on his hind legs. For a brief flicker of a moment, he looked less frightening. The expression in his eyes wasn't rage, but bewilderment.

Next to me, Maya grabbed my hand and yanked me into the undergrowth.

We stayed completely still, not daring to move a muscle as Yellow Eye blundered through the bushes, searching for us. At one moment I could see his claw just inches away from my left arm.

Eventually, he seemed to give up and he turned, folding his wings. We watched with amazement as his vast frame lumbered out of the forest, his tail swishing and his scales glistening in the sunlight.

'I always knew you could do it,' said Dad's voice in my head.

He was right. That was true. But still, I wasn't sure if I'd done the right thing.

'What just happened?' said a shaky voice, and this time it was Adam, not Dad. 'You talked him into leaving. How?'

'You saved our lives, Kon!' said Maya. 'You actually saved our lives!'

'No, I don't think so,' I said, confused. My hands were still shaking. 'I don't think he would have done anything. He only wanted to frighten us and I didn't let him.'

'Are you serious? He's a wild beast!' said Adam. 'He definitely wanted our skins!'

The three of us crawled out of the bushes and found the cart. Apollo and Electra were trembling and we felt pretty shaky too. We comforted the horses, then sat hugging our knees to our chests.

I ran through the events in my head over and over. When I closed my eyes, I could see the dragon's bright scales, which minutes before had been so close I could have touched them. The more I thought about it, the more certain I was that there had been some sort of connection between us.

'He was trying to understand me,' I said aloud, and then wished that I could take it back, it sounded so ridiculous.

But Maya and Adam nodded.

'Maybe there's more to him than we think?' whispered Maya. 'I can't believe we're alive.' She put her hand to her chest and I could tell that her heart was still hammering away like mad, just as mine was.

# 14

Adam eventually calmed Apollo and Electra enough to get us home. They kept stopping, as if to check that Yellow Eye wasn't lurking somewhere. I couldn't believe it when I heard the trumpet call for eight o'clock as we pulled up outside the stables. It felt as though several lifetimes had passed.

Hours earlier, as we'd been setting out, I had dared to imagine us returning as heroes, with people lining the streets celebrating Yellow Eye's departure. But the town was as empty as before, and nobody paid us any attention. We'd ridden in almost complete silence, so it was only when we got the horses to the stables that I asked the question I already knew the answer to.

'He's back in the cave, isn't he?'

'He is,' said Adam sadly.

'Still, thank you for everything,' I said. 'I'm sorry you had to put your life in danger to help us.'

'It wasn't just helping *you*. It would have helped us all if it had worked,' said Adam. 'And that's why it was worth it. Thank you for letting me be a part of it, even if it ended the way that it did. At least I can say that I've tried.'

And then, unexpectedly, he hugged us both, before turning to leave.

'Konrad! Maya!' cried a voice as we crossed the street. We saw Teresa flying out of the bakery.

'There you are!' she shouted, and I could see the relief in her eyes quickly turning to fury. 'Where were you? Where were you?'

'We were with the horses,' I stammered. I glanced at Maya and felt our unspoken agreement not to tell anyone about what had happened unless we absolutely had to.

'What did I say about leaving the house? Do you think different rules apply to you? Do you think you're not in danger? I'm supposed to keep you safe!'

'I'm so sorry,' said Maya. 'We went to see Apollo. We thought we'd be safe, and we didn't think—'

'That's just the thing,' snapped Teresa. 'You can't afford not to think. Please come back now!' And as we marched into the house, she bolted the door tightly behind us.

'I've had the whole street searching for you,' said Teresa. 'I've deliberately put people in danger,' she said, her head in her hands. 'And then I couldn't find Peter and I didn't know what to do. Why can't everyone just be where they promise to be?'

'I'm sorry,' I repeated quietly. 'Please don't be angry. It's my fault. I thought that we could...'

Just then we heard a knock at the door and Peter's voice.

Teresa unbolted the door to let him in.

'Were you looking for me?' he asked and paused when he saw us. We must have made a miserable sight, windswept and dishevelled.

'It's good that you're here,' he said. Unlike Teresa, he wasn't angry at all.

'We took the horses out,' I said. 'They'd been in the stables for weeks. So we took them – Apollo and Electra.'

Peter's gaze travelled from Maya to me. His blue eyes met mine and there was something in them that scared and comforted me. It was as though he knew exactly what had happened. It was almost as if he'd *been* there with us.

'I'm glad you're safe,' he said simply.

'Well, you won't be doing that again, that's for certain,' said Teresa. 'I'll call off the search. Sorry for troubling you, Peter.'

We settled around the table. So far I'd enjoyed working on the books, but this morning had been tense, and we were so shaken and tired that working with Teresa was hard.

She sighed, noticing how quiet Maya was, and I thought that she was going to tell us off again, but her expression softened.

'I'm sorry I shouted,' she said. 'I just – I thought that you'd run away because of what's going on. Only the other day there were reports of a couple of lads who'd fled. You can't blame them. The whole town's gone mad and, honestly, I don't know how long we can go on for.'

'We wouldn't have left without you,' I said

instinctively. The answer came easily. I knew that my place in the world was elsewhere. That I only formed a part of this Konrad, or perhaps he only formed a part of me, but I knew for certain that he wouldn't have abandoned Teresa.

'I thought so,' she said, clasping my hands. 'But, you know, I worried. I sometimes wonder what you might be thinking.'

And her confused, helpless expression reminded me of Mum. Mum, who was light years away back home and with whom I didn't really share a common language. She hadn't known what to expect from me, because I wouldn't tell her anything. I wouldn't say a word to her.

'We're not going anywhere without you,' I repeated to Teresa as the tears fell down her face.

Maybe we should have told her the truth about what we'd done, but the time wasn't right. So instead, we talked about everything except the dragon. Teresa served us leek and onion soup and described her mother's recipe in detail. Then she told us about the dresses her mother had made for the previous queen, and the robes she'd helped her sew for four nights in a row when there had been a royal visit from the King of Prussia.

Though while we tried our best to be interested in the story, all three of us were really listening for the dragon. But all was quiet.

In the late afternoon, we heard a knock on the door and a short, slightly balding man entered, dressed in a uniform and red cloak.

'Good day, Sir Antoni,' said Teresa, brushing down her apron and tidying scattered papers off the floor. 'We weren't expecting you.'

'No. I come bearing instructions from the king in light of recent developments ... and the increasing unpredictability of the situation.'

'Recent developments?' asked Teresa anxiously. 'What's happened?'

Sir Antoni made sure that the door behind him was shut. 'We have received word at the castle that Yellow Eye was seen following a cart into the forest this morning. It's curious and concerning, you'll agree. He's since returned, and he's been standing outside the cave, watchful. What's more, the beast isn't sleeping. The king is worried that he might roam the town, but he hasn't moved. I caught sight of him through the window, and I believe he could be plotting a major attack. Lack of sleep will only increase his intent. The king is at his wits' end and has ordered an evacuation of the castle. It's only thanks to some excellent planning that we managed to get everyone out via the trapdoor in absolute silence.'

'You've all left? And where is the king?'

'He's been transported to his country residence. Now, you may not mention him leaving the castle until it's officially announced. However, we need to arrange transport of the king's books that you currently have in storage. He wants them all with him. He believes they'll be much safer there than in the town. And, of course, you'll soon have to evacuate too. I will organise carts to come and collect the books.'

'When will we have to evacuate?' asked Teresa. I could hear the panic in her voice.

Sir Antoni sighed and seemed to debate whether he should go on. He didn't look at any of us as he spoke.

'The guards will proclaim to all the townsfolk that we must flee Kraków. By midday tomorrow everyone will know. We'll divide ourselves between four different settlements in the north, where we are hopeful our fellow countrymen may take us in, at least until the danger passes.'

'We're leaving?' I asked, hardly believing what I was hearing.

The sense of failure hit me hard. This was it. We'd run out of time.

As Teresa escorted Sir Antoni to the door, Maya whispered to me, 'We have one night left. I have an idea.'

## 15

The evening was spent packing. Teresa pulled leather trunks from the cellar and filled them with clothes. She roasted potatoes and chicken and packed them in jars for the journey. She fretted over the king's precious books, which she wrapped in multiple layers of cloth, so that they wouldn't be damaged during transport. She tried to estimate how much weight a single horse might pull. With my recent experience I could offer her quite a good guess, but I didn't say anything.

'Where is Peter?' Teresa wailed. 'I need his help. I can't do this on my own.'

'He doesn't know yet,' I reminded her. 'Remember – we got a warning from Sir Antoni. Most people won't be told until tomorrow and it will be impossible for them to leave straight away. In fact, if they pack their belongings, they probably won't make a move until evening at the earliest.'

As I said this, I didn't know whether it was true. Perhaps people would grab a few essential belongings and run. Maybe they'd been expecting this announcement and were itching to get away. There was a chance that I was trying to convince myself that we had more time.

When we finally finished packing, it was almost midnight and I fell into bed. I was exhausted and scared, but mostly, I was furious. I pulled the green book from its hiding place and opened the front cover, although I knew there would be no change. It was obvious why. We hadn't followed the original story. I felt mad at Maya for being so protective of the dragon.

The empty second page stared back at me. Was there still a chance? All we had to do was find Skuba. If only I'd asked the boy at the farrier's where he lived. Surely somebody in the neighbourhood would know. And if we couldn't find him, then we needed some sulphur. We could put it into one of

Peter's loaves of bread, or a pie. The more I thought about it, the more convinced I was that this was the only way out. The trouble was that I had no idea where to get sulphur. Maybe Adam would know? Maybe he could help me find Skuba's house?

Adam had shown us where he lived – it was on the same road as the stables. I wasn't sure I would be able to make it without candlelight, but I had to try.

I knew that Teresa would never forgive me, but for the third time I lowered myself down from my bedroom window. I didn't tell Maya, as she'd been so against using any form of violence towards the dragon.

I waited for my eyes to adjust to the shadows and then felt my way down the street, keeping my right hand on the wall of the cottages. I once read that this was the best way to get out of a labyrinth. Luckily, I only needed to get as far as the turning to the stables.

That was when someone charged into me with such force that I almost fell over.

'Owww!' I yelped instinctively, holding my hands out to defend myself.

'Kon? Is that you?'

'Maya?'

'Shush. You'll wake everyone up,' she hissed.

'What are you doing walking around in the middle of the night?' I asked, struggling to keep the annoyance from my voice.

'I could ask you the same thing,' she said, sounding hurt. I felt a pang of guilt as I remembered that if it hadn't been for me, neither of us would be here right now.

'I'm trying to find Adam,' I said.

'Why?'

'So he can help me find Skuba or get some sulphur. We need to kill the dragon once and for all. It's what we were meant to do!'

'Is that what you really think?' she asked coldly.

'Yes,' I said, knowing that she would hate it. 'We must use the method that we know will work for certain – we'll poison him. We should have done it from the beginning. But we'll have to think it through. It doesn't have to be drastic,' I added quickly. 'Maybe we could weaken him just enough to be transported somewhere far, far away.'

'No!' said Maya. 'You wouldn't.' I was surprised to hear the shock in her voice.

'He very nearly killed us. Do I have to remind you? You said yourself you couldn't believe we were still alive.'

'But he didn't.'

'No. But—'

'Please, come with me. You're not that person, Kon. Trust me. I think you should listen to Peter,' she said quietly.

'What do you mean?'

'The night Teresa delivered the completed books, he told us about Galatea and the soothsayers. I guessed that he was telling us we should ask for her help. You said yourself that Yellow Eye was trying to communicate with you. Perhaps Galatea can help us get through to him.'

I leaned against the cold brick of the building behind me and wondered. She'd noticed that the conversation with Peter had been important too. It had played on my mind ever since, but I kept pushing it away. I hated to admit it, but Maya had a point. There was something there – a clue.

'I've just been to the Cloth Hall, Kon,' she said.

'What? You went on your own? Weren't you petrified? Isn't it pitch-black in there?'

'I was awfully scared, but I needed to find Galatea, and I thought that you might try to stop me.'

'I wouldn't...' I began to say, but realised that wasn't true.

'So what happened?'

'I went as soon as I was certain Teresa was asleep. I thought I might not even find it, but I remembered Peter saying it was directly opposite the tower of the Basilica, where the trumpet call comes from. It's a huge building with little arches everywhere. The halls are partly lit by oil lamps, so it wasn't completely black. And there was a light coming from the Basilica. The place had an eerie atmosphere. I thought I could hear the echo of my own breath. At first, I just wandered about to see if there was anyone around. I had a strange feeling that I would be tapped on the shoulder at any moment.'

'So what happened then?'

'Well, I found a set of stairs leading downwards. I could see a dull light coming from there.'

I shuddered at the thought and my anger melted away.

'Oh, Maya. Nobody would have had a clue where you were. What would we have done if something had happened to you?'

'I know, I know,' she said impatiently. 'But I'm OK, and the most important thing is that I was told where to find Galatea. Ever since I met her unexpectedly at Teresa's, I've felt we needed to see her again.'

'How do you know where she is?'

'That's the most amazing part of all! There were two women down there in the Cloth Hall basement. I didn't want to disturb them, because I thought that they could be homeless and sheltering from the dragon. But one of them called out my name!'

'What? How did they know you?'

'I don't know, Kon. But they did. They were gathered around a small fire, sorting through some books. One of them turned to me and said that she was glad I'd come. She said she'd been waiting for me.'

'She'd been waiting for you,' I repeated, not understanding. 'But why? Who are they?'

'They said that they were friends of Peter's and that they were book collectors. They were working hard to save the town's forgotten books – those from the monastery storage rooms, the private collections that people had tried to sell, but couldn't and those brought by foreign merchants to the Cloth Hall. Apparently it had been Peter's idea. They were helping. Peter had told them that these books were precious and that they needed to survive for future generations.'

'He said that?'

'Yes.'

The hope I'd felt deep inside my heart was growing. I couldn't wait to speak to Peter and find out if it was true.

'Come on,' said Maya. 'I know where Galatea is. She's waiting for us.'

I followed Maya down the hill, mesmerised by everything she'd told me. Around us lights from the surrounding houses bled into the dark, people couldn't sleep from worrying about the dragon.

The smoke he breathed out hung in the air like a warning.

We didn't take our usual route into the square. Instead, we turned into a side street and, taking a right, found ourselves on a long, meandering road which led to the back of the huge Basilica. Peter had watched the trumpet player there all those years ago. I felt a peculiar thrill taking in the same view that he had.

Unlike the buildings around it, which stood in shrouded silence, the Basilica had a faint, gentle light shining from the stained-glass windows. It was an unearthly, pink dusty glow, like the blushing sky of sunrise.

'See the two pillars?' asked Maya. 'She lives at the top of the shorter one. The other is where the trumpet sound comes from. Apparently, there's a tiny library in Galatea's pillar. It's the only place in Kraków, other than the Cloth Hall cellars, where the book collectors feel that books are truly safe.'

'Because both buildings are too strong for Yellow Eye to attack?'

'Exactly. The back door should be open. We just need to twist the knob three times.'

'Are you sure you want to do this?' I asked Maya. 'We don't know who Galatea is. She could be mad. Or dangerous.'

'I'm sure,' Maya answered calmly. 'We're going in, Kon. Everything we've done so far has been mad *and* dangerous. But beware, the book collectors told me there are loads of stairs.'

'Loads' turned out to be the understatement of the century. We stopped three times on the way up to get our breath and I counted four hundred and nine stairs in total. At moments, feeling around in the gloom for the wall, it was as if we were lost in a never-ending spiral of doom.

Eventually, the stairs ended and a thin beam of light appeared beneath a small, wooden door.

Maya put her hand up to knock, but before her knuckle even grazed the wood, the door swung open, revealing a squat, hunched figure.

'Come in,' said Galatea in a voice both gentle and unsettling. 'It's a cold night. You mustn't freeze your bones.'

The room was round, but more spacious than I'd expected. In its centre was a dining table, and behind it, a step ladder leading to a higher floor. There was a stove and a wash basin. Otherwise, every surface was covered in books.

They rose in piles from the floor, like strange plants trying to reach sunlight. Large books balanced on top of smaller ones, piles leaned on one another, and there were even books stashed on top of the tiny bed. I recognised some of the folk tales and legends that Dad had read to me. Many of the tomes were leather bound and looked much heavier than the copies I had at home, but when I picked one of them up, it felt light in my hand, like feathered magic.

In the corner, I noticed some rolls of silk in rich blues and purples. My eyes rested on a particular shade of green that reminded me of something.

'You like reading,' said Galatea, observing me carefully.

'Yes,' I admitted.

'And you've spotted something familiar,' she said, touching the green roll of silk fondly with her fingers. That's when I remembered exactly where I'd seen that shade.

'Did you make it? Did you make *The Book of*

*Ancient Legends?*' I asked. My heart leaped with hope. If Galatea had created it, maybe she'd know how we could make the rest of the story return?

'Me?' she asked, her eyes widening with surprise. 'Of course not. I am a rescuer, not a writer. Besides, it's a strange thing to ask. Because the two of you have just spent the last few days making the very book you speak of.'

'No, that's not the one I mean. I'm talking about the green book that I found in the bookshop... Not the one that we worked on with Teresa.'

Galatea poured oil into the pink lamp at the centre of the table and asked calmly, 'Might they not be one and the same? When I rescue the book, all will become clear.'

'Rescue? What do you mean?' asked Maya.

'In the fullness of time, I will retrieve it, rebind it and reignite its magic,' she said, smiling. 'But let's speak no more of the book for now, because you have a much bigger concern. You'll need some fortification before we set out.'

'What? Where are we going?' asked Maya, surprised. 'We've just arrived.'

'To see the dragon, of course,' said Galatea. 'Is this not what you came for?'

She motioned for us to sit on the two chairs closest to us and poured a transparent green liquid from a brass teapot into two ornate glasses.

'Yes,' said Maya. 'You knew?'

'Oh, yes. As well as I know you,' she said, smiling in Maya's direction.

'How?' asked Maya, and her voice shook.

'Oh, I knew you'd come eventually,' said Galatea gently. 'I've been waiting for you. You two are most unusual. You are from here and yet not from here.'

She spread out the fabric of one of her long draping sleeves and held it over the oil lamp at the centre of the table. The light shone through a tiny tear in it, causing a pink shadow, like a star, to dance across the domed ceiling.

'Isn't it a wondrous thing?' she asked. 'A hole. This one is in my sleeve. But there are holes everywhere. Holes, tears, cuts, gaps. It's where the light shines through into the dark. You happened to find a story hole. They're the best kind. I've been looking for them all my life,' she said, sighing and spreading her arms wide.

Amazed, I asked, 'Has anyone else come here? Did you help them get back? Could you help us?'

Galatea put a finger to her lips.

'I can't get you back, Konrad. This is a task for the two of you. And only for you. You must finish your own legend,' she said, raising an eyebrow. 'As for whether there are others, yes. But again, you know.'

'I don't—'

She looked at me, her eyes narrowing, forcing me to think.

'No matter, Konrad. For now, we must do what we must do.'

'Which is what?'

'You will see the dragon. You will get to know him.'

'Oh, we *know* him. We know him too well. That's not the problem,' I said, suddenly furious. I didn't have time for riddles. 'We need to destroy him! Or drive him out of the town. So either you'll help us, or we'll leave!' My voice echoed around the circular walls, bouncing back like a raging storm.

'I'll try,' she said calmly, then walked over to Maya, and held the lamp directly in front of her. She sat in the chair opposite and grasped Maya's shaking hands between her own.

'I'm glad that you are here, my child,' she said softly. 'You have an important role to play. Have you noticed yourself becoming stronger recently? You must believe in yourself.'

She turned towards me. 'Drink your tea. And let's begin your important journey.'

I looked at the green liquid doubtfully, but Maya had already drunk hers and she motioned to me to do the same. I swallowed it and felt a pleasant burning sensation. My tiredness seemed to vanish and my thoughts were clear and more focused than they'd been in days.

Galatea took her pink glow lamp, shut the door to her tower and walked down the stairs at a surprisingly brisk pace. We struggled to keep up. The lamp was easily ten times brighter than any of the oil lamps in Teresa's house. When we reached the bottom, its light illuminated the interior of the Basilica, and I stopped, entranced. I don't know what I'd expected, but it wasn't this.

The altar, the walls, the pews, the pillars… It was more magnificent than any building I'd ever seen. It looked like every element had taken months, if not years, of careful planning. The wooden pillars were decorated in gold. There were figures of people carved with such detail that I could make out their different facial expressions. The coloured stained-glass windows glimmered with reflected light. I was mesmerised by the floor beneath my feet, which was a mosaic of carefully assembled bricks. Then I raised my head and I saw it for the first time.

'The heavens,' Galatea said quietly, directing the beam of light towards the ceiling. Maya gasped. In the dusty pink beam, it was impossible to tell where the building ended and where the sky began.

'It's as if there's no roof,' I whispered. In fact, I hadn't realised that the starry sky was the work of some genius artist and not the real thing.

'The painter was in love with stars,' said Galatea. 'He wanted to show us that the constellations are something that we all have in common. It was enjoyed by so many who came before us, and people living centuries into the future will also gaze at its splendour.'

A memory came to me. Mum, Dad and I in the garden at Ocean Drive. It had been a long, sunny day, and we were lying on the grass, staring up at the night sky. I was five or six and I couldn't get my head around what caused stars to shine.

'It's because they are so hot,' Dad had said. 'There are loads of reactions going on inside them. The reactions are so big that the stars continue to shine long after they die.'

'Wow,' I'd replied. 'That's why we can still see them so many years later.'

That was when I'd spotted a shooting star and made a wish that nothing would ever change. The moment was perfect, and I could never imagine feeling any happier.

'Come on. We have no time to marvel,' Galatea said abruptly, and the image splintered and faded.

As we left the Basilica, and walked alongside her on the cobbled streets, I was keen to know more about her plan. It was obvious that she had one.

'What are we going to do when we get to the castle?' I asked outright.

'I'm going to help you to communicate with Yellow Eye,' she said simply. 'I think it's important that you tell him exactly how you feel.'

'You reckon that will help?'

'In more ways than you can possibly imagine.'

Her answer wasn't what I expected, but then, what did I think was going to happen? That she would cast a spell or a curse on the dragon? If that was the case, she would have done it long ago. Maybe there *was* something in the idea of speaking directly with Yellow Eye. After all, he had listened and obeyed me in the forest. At least he'd seemed to.

'Where did you learn to speak dragon-tongue?' asked Maya, falling into step with Galatea. 'Is it a difficult language?'

She considered the question. 'It's not a language, not in the way that you understand. It's gestures and sounds. It's about tuning into one another's emotions. You'll see.'

'We should be firm but fair with him,' Maya whispered to me. 'Don't get angry.'

I almost laughed. This was the dragon that we were talking about.

# 16

Galatea was surprisingly fast on her feet, and within minutes, we were standing outside the cave that I had grown to know so well.

'How do we wake him?' I asked.

'Like this,' said Galatea, putting two fingers in her mouth. She let out a high-pitched whistle.

When nothing happened, she tried again, louder this time. I was conscious of lights appearing in the windows of the buildings behind us. We were waking our fellow townspeople, but not the dragon.

And then the ground shifted beneath my feet and a plume of smoke rose from the cave. Yellow Eye emerged from his lair, his sharp-tipped tail swinging menacingly. His magnificent fiery scales glowed in the beam cast by Galatea's lamp. I smelled his familiar musky breath and the memory of early that morning came flooding back.

He lurched forward in a single, swift movement and spread his wings as if he was about to launch into the air. He was showing us who was boss. Then he glared at me, his giant jaws yawned open, and he shrieked. The sound was so shrill and loud and close that I felt I was shattering into a thousand pieces. I stared back into his yellow eyes, and anger surged through me. This was the beast that had come close to killing us, that held Kraków at its mercy, that had eaten all the food and was about to drive the townspeople from their homes.

'Tell him,' I said to Galatea. 'Tell him that he has to leave now or he will regret it. He has done enough! We hate him!'

Maya pulled at my sleeve. 'Konrad, no —'

But Galatea had already begun speaking. What came out were sounds unlike anything I'd ever heard. These were roars and high-pitched wails and shrieks that didn't seem human. I could see that the dragon had understood.

His eyes blazed and he screamed a hot white fury

as fire scorched the ground. I hadn't imagined such pure, instant rage. His temper matched my own.

'Tell him that nobody wants him here! That we hate what he's done to the town and to everyone who lives here!'

'Don't…' Maya shouted, but her words were drowned as Galatea relayed my own.

The dragon's ears pricked as he listened. He was soaking up my anger with every pore of his being.

'Tell him that we won't forget what he did to Sikora's farm! And that he won't be getting any more food! Tell him that everyone's leaving the town because of him, hoping they will never set eyes on him again.'

The dragon's giant, oily nostrils flared, and smoke began to curl out of them – a thick, black plume that made my eyes smart.

I could see that I was making the situation worse. Instead of trying to reason with the dragon like I'd done that morning, to coax him from the town, here I was pouring out the hatred that had been trapped inside me. I knew that the consequences could be bad, but now I'd started, I couldn't stop.

I looked at Galatea. She nodded at me to carry on, and when I didn't, she came closer and held my hands between hers. I realised then that she knew. She'd known all along. I could feel the last glowing ball of anger pulsating in the pit of my stomach, like the words that had been desperate to spill when I'd met Maya.

'Tell him that this is his last chance! He must leave the town and never come back! At least then he would have done a good thing. And everyone can get back to their families and their jobs and their lives – and be happy!'

The dragon's eyes locked with mine. Without warning, he reared on his hind legs, his vast wings outspread and an enormous shot of flame reached so close that its heat licked my face.

'Run!' screamed Maya, but we couldn't. It was too late. With an earth-shattering roar, Yellow Eye lunged at us. I tumbled, with my hands over my head and ears, bracing for impact.

I waited for the fire to burn my clothes and skin and to feel the massive weight of the dragon crushing me. I'd never experienced fear like it. It was so great that it seemed to rush from me. I felt my face wet with tears.

Someone grasped my shoulder and I heard Maya. She was singing. It was the song I'd heard on the beach, that first day I'd met her. That beautiful, otherworldly tune rang through the air, and Maya's voice didn't falter, even for a second. The sound soothed Galatea's angry wails, which had been my own despair. Maya's voice was pure and carefree, like the wind. It pierced through my fear.

As she sang, the atmosphere changed. I felt a sudden lightness. I dared to open my eyes and lifted myself into a kneeling position.

What I saw seemed unbelievable. Yellow Eye was sitting less than five metres away, his front claws resting in the dirt directly next to my leg. My gaze fell on the footprint it had made, which looked so familiar that I wanted to cry out.

He no longer resembled the furious creature that moments before had shrieked at us and breathed fire. Instead, he seemed comforted after experiencing something horrible.

Yellow Eye looked calm. He looked sad. He looked forlorn. He looked familiar.

'Who are you?' I found myself asking.

But he gave no answer.

When Maya's song drew to a close, she pulled me gently by the elbow and we slowly edged backwards. Galatea was nowhere in sight. She had vanished the moment she was no longer needed. She'd done what she set out to do – she'd helped me get rid of the anger, the fury and the sadness that had lain inside me for so long. And she'd shown me that Yellow Eye and I – we were not so different. In fact, we were one and the same. And yet ... he and I were both still here.

Perhaps there wasn't a way out of the legend? Perhaps we'd missed our chance to find Skuba and we would be forever trapped?

'It was spectacular, what happened back there,' Peter said, hugging us both. 'What are you going to do now?'

'It was our last chance,' I told him, and I couldn't stop the tears falling. 'I messed it up, though. And now there's nothing that anyone can do.'

'It didn't look like you'd messed it up to me,' he said. 'You have soothed a very wounded soul. And you learned a lot in the process. In fact, I feel that you know more about Yellow Eye than anyone else in Kraków.'

His words gave me a grain of hope. I trusted him completely.

'But what good is that if we can't get rid of him?' I asked.

'Well, he hasn't left yet, but you understand him now and that's so important. Come on, tell me the facts that you've gathered. Let's go through them one by one. There will be clues, I'm sure.'

I exhaled slowly. This was what I needed to hear.

'He eats insanely huge amounts of food. More than the town can keep up with,' said Maya quietly. 'And it seems that he's furious if you try to trick him. I think he's very intelligent. What impression do you get, Kon?'

I realised I knew exactly what Yellow Eye wanted.

'He's living in a parallel universe,' I said. 'And nobody's listening.'

Maya looked at me questioningly, so I explained further.

'He wants to communicate with those around him but he can't. He's a lonely creature in a strange land, trying to stay alive. He doesn't fit in here. There's not enough food and everyone's frightened of him. It makes him frightened too. He just wants someone to understand him, and to console him.'

And then a thought occurred to me.

'Maya's song soothed him. And, Peter, do you remember what you told us about him trampling the Sikora farm?'

'Remind me,' he said, although he knew exactly what I meant.

'That the farmer's daughter was singing her baby to sleep in the outhouse.'

'Exactly. And why do you think that's important?'

'It must have reminded him of something. And Maya's song today must have brought back memories too.'

'Do you think so? He looked so peaceful as I was singing,' said Maya. 'Almost happy.'

'Even from a distance I could sense his anger leaving him,' Peter agreed, smiling at me. 'Maya seems to have that effect. I think the two of you need to show him that you understand and that you're on his side.'

'But how will we tell him?' I asked desperately. 'Galatea's gone.'

'You don't need anyone but yourselves,' said Peter. 'Bring your honesty, Kon, and Maya will bring her incredible voice.'

'Let's go,' I said urgently, getting up from the chair.

We were at the door when I turned. 'Will you come with us? Please come.'

Peter nodded, and as I ran outside, I'm sure I heard him say, 'I wouldn't miss it for the Milky Way.'

So the three of us walked back up the hill. Morning was breaking, and the warm sun would soon take up its reign in the sky.

A few stragglers remained in the street, watching the cave from a distance.

'It's them. They're back,' two sisters said excitedly. 'That's the girl whose song stopped the dragon,' one of them said to her mother. 'He's still there,' she told us, 'although I think he's fallen asleep. You're not going to wake him, are you?'

'Let's see what happens,' I said, as we carried on our way.

They were right. It looked as if Yellow Eye was dozing. He was curled into a ball, his giant tail tucked around his head. I walked close to him, so close that I could see his glistening skin and the wrinkles around his nostrils. He didn't seem to be in a deep sleep, as one of his eyes was only half-closed and his tail was twitching gently.

The three-pronged claw with its long, curled nails rested on the ground in front of me, and something compelled me to stroke it.

The dragon's half-open eye opened further. He didn't move but he looked at me as if to say that I should keep going.

Then Maya began to sing. It was a song I hadn't heard before. It was beautiful and soulful, and I noticed that there was something else, a spark of hope. Yellow Eye heard it too, because he blinked and gazed attentively at Maya, as if remembering something.

Peter helped Maya on to a broken pillars so that she could project her voice. I noticed Galatea, wrapped in a coloured shawl, quietly watching us from a distance with a mixture of pride and fascination.

Her presence only made Maya's voice stronger. She sang and sang, directing the song straight at Yellow Eye.

And then I felt the claw beneath my hand move as the dragon scrambled into a standing position. Still watching Maya, he let out a sound that was high and melodic and hopeful – and it was followed by another and another. Maya and I looked at each other in amazement when we realised what was happening. Yellow Eye was singing. His voice got louder and clearer in an incredible harmony with Maya's.

The song sent me on a journey of different emotions, from anger through sadness, all the way to hope, and even joy. It was as if my own internal universe was suddenly coming back to life.

And then the strangest thing yet happened. A third voice joined in, almost like an echo of the dragon's. It had risen so much in volume that it had probably woken everyone in town. But as I listened, I realised that it was separate – it came from somewhere else.

Yellow Eye turned towards the mountains, far beyond the forest. That was where it came from.

He moved in its direction, as if not daring to believe that it was really true.

The voice soared, carried by the wind. I didn't speak dragon-tongue, but I could sense that it was responding to Yellow Eye.

'It's more than one voice,' Maya whispered.

She was right. Multiple voices rose across the mountains. The dragon belonged to these voices, and they belonged to him.

'Keep singing to them,' Maya urged. 'Make sure they hear you.'

Yellow Eye hesitated. He looked at us and there was longing in his eyes, as if he was sad. He lowered his head, and I was shocked to see that he wanted us to touch it. I stroked the rough, fiery, lizard-like skin, which was warm and surprisingly soft, unlike the sharp smooth coldness of his claw.

He was saying 'thank you' and 'goodbye'.

'No, thank *you*,' I whispered to him. 'Get back safely. You can do it.'

And we watched as he walked in the direction of the river once again. We followed at a distance, curious to see where he would go. I felt somehow devastated that he was leaving just as we were getting to know him.

Yellow Eye continued to sing as he crossed the bridge. I tracked him as he pressed on through the fields towards the forest, never once stopping to look back. He disappeared among the densely packed trees and all was still.

Maya held my elbow, and we both stood on the riverbank, not daring to believe what had happened. Yellow Eye could still be heard faintly in the distance. Otherwise, all that was left of him were his footprints in the sand.

18

Word about the dragon's departure spread quickly through the town. A crowd had watched the whole scene from afar, and in no time told their friends who passed it on to everyone they knew.

There were those who doubted that Yellow Eye was gone for good and worried that he would soon return when he got hungry. Only Peter and Galatea were completely calm, as though they knew that Kraków was finally free. I trusted their instincts.

When, by evening, there was still no sign of him, the king returned to the castle and ordered a feast in the grounds. The food, which would normally have been reserved for the dragon, was brought for everyone to enjoy.

The people who lived closest to the castle, and hadn't dared to leave their houses for weeks, hurried out with tables and chairs. Musicians set up their instruments outside the dragon's empty cave.

Maya, Teresa and Peter were gathered in the kitchen debating how many chairs they needed to bring. The milk for the hot chocolate was bubbling on the stove and Teresa was making poppyseed cake.

'I still can't believe what you did,' she exclaimed over and over, as she stirred the mixture. 'All this time you were plotting! I should have known.'

She pretended to be cross that we hadn't let her in on our secret, but she couldn't hide how happy she was.

'Our song reminded him that he could sing too,' said Maya. 'I think Galatea knew it would. And when he did, his family and friends answered, and he could make his way home to them.'

'It was *your* song,' I corrected her. 'You sang it to a wild, fierce creature and you didn't even look scared.'

'It was scary. Until I realised that he wasn't what we thought he was. And that he was frightened himself. But also, it wasn't just me. We'd never have got to where we did without you.'

'It took a lot of courage from you both,' said Peter. 'Now are you ready? The king wants to meet you.'

The celebrations lasted throughout the evening and into the night. There was music and dancing and shows put on by street magicians. In the middle of the celebrations, Maya and I were swept up by the crowd and carried down the dancefloor on their shoulders.

Later, when we'd accepted congratulations from hundreds of people, I took a breath and sat down to talk to Adam who wanted to know exactly what had happened.

'You didn't give up,' he said, patting me on the back. 'Who knew that would work on him? And there we were, trying to drive him out with food in the cart.'

'It seems mad now, but it needed to be done. We had to see what worked. So you really helped us.'

'I'll have a story to tell until I'm a very old man!'

Out of the corner of my eye, I saw Maya talking to Galatea. The old lady hugged her close, and it was as if they were falling into a familiar embrace. I overheard her say, 'Maya, you must continue with the singing. It has been your gift, ever since you were a child. You must nourish it and do everything you can to develop your voice.'

Just before the sun went down, the king appeared on the stage outside the dragon's cave and asked us to join him. He was a powerful-looking man. I couldn't imagine him ever being scared of anyone or anything, but I realised now that appearances could be deceiving.

'You don't need me to tell you,' he said, and his eyes were glistening, 'that you did something unbelievably courageous this morning. You freed us. Thanks to you we can leave our houses and live our lives once more. And you taught us a very important lesson. We'd misjudged Yellow Eye. To us he was a beast to be feared, full of fury, without a soul. We were wrong. He deserved to be understood, in the way that every one of us deserves to be listened to and appreciated. So, Maya and Konrad, I thank you from the bottom of my heart for teaching us that. Please accept these small gifts as tokens of our appreciation,' he said, handing us each a gold coin. I noticed that on one side there was an intricate crest, and on the other a tiny image of the Basilica with its two very special towers. I put it in my pocket for safe keeping.

I squeezed Maya's hand tight as the entire town cheered around us.

Later, long past midnight, when the party was in full swing, Maya pulled me aside.

'Let's walk to the river,' she said. My head was reeling from the crowds and the noise.

There were fewer people here, although a couple of youngsters had lit fires further down the beach and were roasting sausages. In the light of Maya's lantern, I could still make out Yellow Eye's footprints in the sand. It was a beautiful night. The full moon was reflecting on the water, and behind us, the illuminated castle looked like a fairy tale.

'Do you think he found his family?' Maya whispered.

'Definitely.'

'He was searching for them all along, wasn't he? That's why he was so scared. You know, I get the sense that he was much younger than everyone thought. Maybe he still needed them to support him.'

'True.'

'Kon?'

'Yeah?'

'I was so afraid and desperate to get back to our world. But now, I'm kind of glad that it happened. Is that a crazy thing to say?'

I turned and looked at her, amazed. Because it was as if she had read my thoughts.

'Not at all.'

'You know Galatea? She's – well, she's my avó. I was going to say that she's *like* my avó, but there isn't any need for the *like*. Do you understand what I'm saying?'

But before I could answer, there were footsteps behind us and I turned to see Peter. Without his work clothes, he looked different – freer and happier. He sat beside us and took his shoes off, wriggling his toes as if wanting to feel the sand in between them.

'I've never danced so much in my life,' he said. 'Teresa didn't want to stop.'

Maya looked meaningfully at me, as if to say that we would continue our conversation later.

'Isn't it amazing that he reacted to a song?' she asked Peter.

'Songs are extremely powerful.'

'I never thought they were until now,' she admitted. 'I thought that they were silly, you know, compared to other important things that people do.'

'Well, you only need to look back there,' he said, motioning towards the castle where a singer entertained the dancing crowds. 'He isn't nearly as good as you and look at the effect that he's having. Your song gave a dragon its voice back. Always remember that. He needed his voice to reconnect with those who love him.'

He looked at me as he said those last words and they hit me square in the centre of my chest.

'Feel like dipping your feet in?' he asked, grinning at us.

I hesitated. The river had always looked so rough when I'd seen it from the shore. But Maya was already pulling her shoes off.

'Come on, what are you waiting for?'

And I was taking my shoes off too and jumping off the rocky bank. The water was cool. I gazed up at the stars. They seemed brighter tonight.

'Isn't it awesome that the Milky Way is so clear here?' I asked. I'd never seen it like this from our garden in Ocean Drive.

Peter was quiet for a moment. And then he said: 'It's where the lights bleed into the darks. Sometimes you need to let them, my intrepid explorer.'

The breath stopped in my throat. But I'm not sure why it did, because on some level, I'd always known. I'd recognised his eyes the moment that I'd seen this version of him, in this strange, medieval town. I turned to embrace him, to jump on his back shouting, 'It's me! We're together again!'

But even as I turned, the glow from the castle faded, and I found I couldn't see anything. I felt the cool water circling my feet in eddies and smelled the sweet chamomile that filled the castle gardens. I could still taste Teresa's poppyseed cake on the tip of my tongue. It was then that the memory returned unexpectedly.

Dad and I were standing in the water, a few

metres away from where I'd later find the dragon print. We were searching for the long snouted seahorse, which we'd seen by chance while we'd been fishing.

I was beckoning Dad to come over quietly. And then he'd tripped on something and crashed into the water like an elephant, causing such a racket that even the nearby seagulls flew off in a huff, not to mention the poor seahorses.

The fall had been so spectacular that we'd stood laughing for a good five minutes. That image of the two of us – Dad trying to regain his serious explorer face, and me, holding on to our underwater camera, doubled over laughing – began to fuzz over slightly, but the feeling of pure happiness remained.

I'd had to leave Dad and the seahorses because I'd promised Jomar that we'd meet for an afternoon game of football, but I hadn't really wanted to go. I'd lingered for a moment, suspended. And then I'd walked towards the beach, shaking myself dry.

And somewhere within the deep dragon cave of my mind I knew that in my current form, I was also leaving – that I would leave before I got a chance to tell Peter … before I could jump on Dad's back… There was no more before. There was only the present and it was calling to me.

# 19

When I opened my eyes, I was still staring up at a starry sky, but something had changed.

Next to me, I heard a cough. I turned to see Maya pulling herself into a sitting position.

She was wearing her bright blue dress with the yellow sunflowers, but it was mud-stained at the bottom, as if she'd been wading through water. And then I spotted the print next to her foot, with the three-pronged claw– the exact shape and size as those made by Yellow Eye on the river's edge.

Maya gazed around uncertainly.

'We're back,' she whispered. 'Kon, we're actually back!'

And then she hugged and hugged me, until there was barely any breath left in either of us.

'You remember it all, right?' she asked me. 'Please tell me you remember it.'

'Yeah, of course,' I said. 'We helped Yellow Eye get home.'

My head was whirring with thoughts of the dragon, and Peter and Dad and the print. Had we truly left medieval Kraków behind?

I breathed in the cool, salty night air. Next to us, the waves splashed on the shingle, and I could see the silhouette of the lighthouse in the distance. Beyond that was Ocean Drive, with its tidy lawns and parked cars. It had been days since we'd seen a car. But what had happened in our world? Had we been gone for days too? My heart sank at the thought of how much Mum must have been worrying.

'Maya, we have to go home,' I said urgently. 'Your parents and my mum – they have no clue…'

I stopped suddenly. A group of people with torches were coming along the beach in our direction.

'Maya?' called a man's panicked voice.

'Oh my goodness, is that them? Can you see Konrad?' It was Mum. Her voice tugged at something deep inside me. I scrambled to my feet and started running towards her.

She looked wonderful – tired, hair dishevelled, more anxious than ever, but otherwise the same as I'd last seen her. She was even wearing the same worn blue jumper that smelled faintly of the sea.

'I'm sorry,' I said, wrapping my arms around her. 'I didn't mean to scare you. We just… We ended up somewhere we hadn't planned to go.'

I knew it wasn't wise to mention where. At least, not now. Not yet. Mum was hugging me tight. She pulled me back momentarily to look at me with amazement. 'You're speaking, Kon.' I realised that it was the first time I'd managed a proper sentence to her since Dad died.

'Oh, Kon. I was beginning to freak out,' said Mum, her tears running freely. 'I went to the bookshop when you hadn't come back for dinner, and it was unlocked. The lights were on, but you were nowhere in sight. I thought maybe you were in the stockroom, but when I couldn't find you, I was scared. I rang Stephen and he told me that you were there when he left which made me panic more.'

'Were you waiting for me?'

'I waited for a while, and then Mr and Mrs Rocha arrived. Maya had told them that she was going to "a place full of stories" with you, so they asked around and found our bookshop. They'd already searched the beach, knowing the two of you liked to hang out there.'

'How long have you been looking?' I asked.

'Well, I got to A Likely Story at five-thirty and now it's almost nine, so a long time, Kon.'

How was it possible that we'd only been missing for such a short time? Days had been packed into those brief few hours.

Maya embraced a woman with flowing, dark hair just like hers. A tall, thin man with glasses was standing next to them. They spoke in a mixture of Portuguese and English, but it was obvious how relieved Maya's parents were to see her.

'I was so scared,' her dad kept saying, as he embraced her. Then, as we started walking back towards the street, his tone turned more serious.

'Maya, you can't do that again. It's totally irresponsible,' he said. 'From now on, you won't be allowed on the beach without one of us with you.'

I watched as she stopped walking and faced him. I knew that the other Maya would have apologised and hung her head. But this wasn't the old, meek Maya. This Maya had helped a dragon find his family through the power of song and freed a whole town.

'No,' she said, as I high-fived her in my head. 'I'm sorry I didn't send a message and that I didn't come home when I should have had, but it wasn't my fault – truly. I love hanging out here. I've learned so much about this place. I know all the newts in the marsh pools, and the leeches, and I've counted the different plants that grow. Do you know that there are thirty-seven different species living here, even though people call it a desert? It's where I sing out loud, without being embarrassed of you hearing, and it's where I met Kon. We're friends and I want to spend more time with him.'

Her dad was taken aback by her reply and had no idea what to say.

'You're embarrassed of your singing?' asked her

mum. 'But we love hearing it. You should sing to us more – you know, after you've finished lessons.'

'About that,' Maya said, her voice growing more confident, 'I don't think home-schooling is for me. I was thinking that I could go to Kon's school? They apparently have a great music department.'

'Well…' her mum began. 'If it's something that would make you happy, then we can definitely discuss it.'

'We haven't finished deciding what the consequences of your behaviour tonight will be,' replied her dad. But I could tell that the conversation was shifting and that changes were about to happen in Maya's life.

'We'd better be heading home,' said Mum.

'Will you come round tomorrow?' I whispered to Maya as we said goodbye to her and her family. 'That's my house. The green one.'

'I'll try,' she promised.

I'd never been so glad to sit at the kitchen table with Mum. As she boiled the milk and began to make the hot chocolate, I had a flashback to Teresa doing the very same thing over a hot stove in medieval Kraków. It was as though I was watching myself from the outside, gazing in.

'So what really happened, Kon?' Mum asked.

'Maya and I got lost in a book,' I answered honestly.

'Oh. Which one?'

'It was *The Book of Ancient Legends* – you know, the one Dad always used to read to me.'

'Ah, I thought you would find Dad in the bookshop. He's always in there,' she said, smiling. 'You know, I've been asking him questions when I need to work something out. Sometimes I managed to get it right and I know it's because he helped me.'

'Maya says that everything in nature leaves a little bit of itself behind. It rubs off on the world around it.'

'She's right, I'm sure. She's a clever girl. It's not just true of nature, though. I think people leave parts of themselves behind in the things and people they love.'

'Yeah, I … I can see that.'

'Your dad is in so much of you too, Kon,' she said quietly. 'He would have been happy to see you meet someone you can share all the things you love with.'

And because of the way she said it, I could read between the words and knew exactly what she meant.

'That's not because I don't want to share them with you, Mum,' I told her. 'I just… Until recently, I couldn't do it. It was as if something in me was stuck. But now it's been unblocked – I'm sorry I can't explain it better, but I promise you I'll keep trying.'

I wanted to tell her all the things that I'd been holding back since Dad had gone. But I would have to do it gradually. And I knew what I wanted to start with.

'There's something in particular I want to show you,' I told her. 'And that's a print that I've discovered on the rocks by the sea, you know – where you found us.'

'Wow, what sort of print?'

'It's huge. I don't know which giant beast it could have belonged to, but I have a good idea.'

'Well, I can't wait to see it, Kon. We can go tomorrow.'

She took a sip of her drink as I debated whether to ask another important question.

'Mum … is there any chance that you would reconsider selling A Likely Story?'

The smile that had been playing on her face disappeared.

'Oh, Kon. I don't know – I think it's for the best. I'm not your dad. I can't quite do it justice and I think the people who come to buy books can feel it. It would be better off in someone else's hands.'

'What if I helped? On weekends and some days after school? I have ideas for what would make it really awesome. Could you give me a chance? Maybe just a month?'

Mum raised her eyebrows in surprise. This was more enthusiasm than she'd had from me in the last six months combined. I wouldn't have blamed her if she said no.

'Well … we don't have a buyer yet, so let's see what we can do in a month, shall we?'

'Fantastic,' I said, going to hug her. 'I promise you won't regret this.'

## 20

Since Maya and I had returned home, my two universes divided by 4 November were not so separate any more. There were still bad days when I missed Dad terribly and I wanted to think about him instead of speaking to anyone, but they were fewer. And I no longer felt guilty for the good moments, when Maya and I laughed at Amarelo bobbing his head up and down like a rapper, or when I managed to score a goal against Ravi – the first in nearly six months. I let the light moments bleed into the dark ones.

At the end of the Easter holidays, three really important things happened, which I wouldn't have imagined possible even two weeks before.

The first was to do with the claw print, which I

showed to Mum next day. Maya and I took her to our spot on the rock and she studied it carefully. I had no idea that she would be interested. But then she told us the story of how she and Dad had met, which I couldn't believe I'd never heard before.

It had been in the Natural History Museum in the dinosaur gallery under the Diplodocus skeleton that used to be there.

'We were both admiring it,' she said. 'I was on my own. I'd taken a longer lunch break – I needed to be away from my desk for a while and I'd decided the museum was just the place. I'd heard about the Diplodocus skeleton, but I'd never seen it. And then I saw this man, also on his own, studying the skeleton closely, as if he wanted to remember every single bone.

'And that was Dad?'

'That was Dad. He saw me looking and he said: "How many of these do you think haven't been discovered yet?" I asked what he meant, and he explained: "We have almost the complete skeleton of one, and we know about hundreds of other species. But I reckon it's the tip of the iceberg.

What if there are more that we don't have a clue about?"'

'That's the first thing he said to you?' I asked, amazed.

'Pretty much.'

'It sounds like he should have studied them,' said Maya.

'I think he loved reading and books just a bit more than he loved dinosaurs. But it was a close second,' said Mum, laughing. 'How would you feel about telling someone about this print? We could contact the local paper and send them a photo.'

I thought about it for a long time. Because the print felt like my secret and Dad's. Even though he'd never seen it in real life, I'd spoken to him so much about it. And I didn't know whether I wanted others to know about it. But Maya knew too and Mum. In my head, I asked Dad what he thought, and I felt him giving me the thumbs up.

The story appeared in the paper the following week, and then it made the national news. A specialist research team came to take measurements and more photos, and Professor Jim Jacobsen, the most famous dinosaur expert in the UK, came to investigate the print himself, and Mum, Maya and I got to meet him. He was short and balding, with thick rimmed glasses and a bristly moustache.

Of course, the first question I asked was:

'Which species do you think made the print?'

'I've been asking myself the same question,' he admitted. 'My guess, as I'm sure yours would be too, is that it comes from some species of Megalosaurus, but there are a few quirks here that I would like to investigate further.'

Dad would have given anything to have a chance to meet the professor, so I knew I couldn't let this opportunity pass. There was something else that I needed to ask him. The answer would probably be no, but it was worth a shot.

'Professor, do you think you could give a talk at our bookshop? We have all your books in stock in our special dinosaur section.'

'Kon,' Mum started, 'I'm sure that the professor has far better—'

But I could see by the way he smiled that he seemed keen on the idea.

'I would be glad to,' he said. 'Shall we set a date?'

And we did, for three weeks away. The professor even promised to bring a couple of the fossils from his private collection.

The second most incredible thing that happened was that Maya joined our class. She had persuaded her parents that she needed to meet more people and they decided to give regular school a try. On her first lunchtime, I took her straight to Mr Phillips to ask whether she could join the choir. He agreed to an audition the following day and I came along to watch. He was more excited by what he'd heard than I'd predicted.

'Maya,' he said, trying to choose the right words, 'you have a very rare talent. We need to hone it and make sure that you put it to good use. It goes without saying that you can be part of the choir, and I hope you might audition for our musical production this summer. It's a medley of songs from all over the world. I know that you'd be brilliant!'

I was so pleased when he said that, because I knew that Maya needed to hear it from someone other than me and Peter – someone who really knew music. She took him up on his offer and I could just feel that the role would be perfect for her. She'd not only been to so many different *places* in the world, but her voice had made an impact in a totally different *time*.

Maya settled into school quickly. I introduced her to Jomar and Ravi, who were really welcoming, although I'm not sure they had that much in common with her. I suspected they were both secretly shocked that I was now good friends with a girl.

There was someone who was keen to point it out and, of course, that person was Luke.

'Here he comes, the famous dinosaur hunter,' he said sarcastically at lunch on our first day back after the holidays, but Maya threw him such a look that he went quiet.

And then something compelled me to stand up and walk over to his table.

'Is it OK if I sit down?' I asked. He nodded in surprise. Noah pulled a face, but I ignored him.

'I wanted to say sorry for seeming like a bad friend and not speaking to you since – well, since

4 November. It wasn't anything to do with you. It was everything to do with Dad. I wasn't myself without him.'

Luke watched me, but he didn't say anything.

'Anyway, I totally get it if you think this claw print stuff is stupid, but there's going to be a small event at Dad's bookshop with the professor – you know the one Dad was always talking about?'

'Yeah, I remember,' he said quietly. 'He loved that guy.'

'It would be awesome if you came,' I said. 'Dad would have wanted you to be there.'

I couldn't read Luke's expression as I got up, but I hoped that something between us had changed.

Next day, the head teacher, Mr Brendan, made an announcement in assembly about how proud the school was of my discovery, and mentioned the professor coming to A Likely Story in early May.

'I would encourage as many of you as possible to go,' he said. 'It will be an incredibly interesting talk.'

A week or so before the event, I took Maya to the bookshop so that we could make a plan. After moving around the central book tables, we saw that there would be plenty of space to seat people. We went down to the basement to see how many chairs we had.

I was in the middle of counting when Maya whispered, 'No way.' I turned to see her holding a familiar-looking book, bound in green silk. Gold dragons danced along its edge. The title was there in bold, elaborate letters: *The Book of Ancient Legends*. She handed it to me, and I opened the cover, my heart beating wildly. The pages were brimming with words. I noticed the familiar gold borders, and the carefully drawn images. I ran my fingers along the familiar calligraphy. I found the image of the bee that I'd painstakingly worked on. There was no doubt that it was *our* book, except there was one additional legend, at the very beginning. I remembered Galatea's words. And then I began to read:

*The Legend of Wawel Castle*

The opening of the legend was familiar. I could recite the words by heart as Dad had read them to me so many times. But Maya's finger pointed to a section that I'd spotted too.

*When it seemed that everything was lost and the people of Kraków were going to be destroyed, two young scribes, a boy and a girl, confronted the dragon. But rather than attempting to kill him, like those who had come before, they tried to lead him out of the town with a trail of food.*

*Sadly, their plan didn't work and the dragon returned. They did not give up. With the help of a soothsayer, the boy spoke, pouring out his anger and frustration at what Yellow Eye had done to the inhabitants of Kraków. The dragon was enraged. Then the girl began to sing, to calm the raging beast. Her beautiful voice had an unexpected effect. The dragon joined in the song. His voice carried over the mountain, where it was heard by his family, who called to him to come home.*

*And with that, Yellow Eye picked himself up and left the town once and for all. A huge celebratory feast was held, and the boy and girl departed as heroes, safe in the knowledge that they'd succeeded in not just taming, but also helping the dragon.*

'Unbelievable,' I whispered to Maya.

'How did this get here?' she said, turning the book over in her hands.

'Teresa must have added it. Maybe the king commissioned her to do it?'

'And then Galatea must have rescued it and bound it in green silk.'

'The main question is – why is it here now?' But even as I asked, I already knew the answer.

Dad.

Maya and I spent ages helping Mum prepare the bookshop for the professor's visit. We moved the furniture, bought new plants to make everything look a bit more cheerful, and even put up a special screen so he could show a presentation of his research. The place had been transformed.

'This is an incredible space for events,' said Maya. 'If this goes well, maybe you could invite authors and other interesting speakers.'

'We could run a book club too,' I said. 'People could vote for the books they want to read in advance. I could help set it up on our website. We've been learning about how to use survey programmes in IT.'

I could tell that Mum was delighted and probably a bit overwhelmed with all the suggestions, but I'm pretty sure she liked us being involved.

'Well, let's see how today goes,' she said.

I put my hands in my pockets and nervously waited for the first people to turn up. All of a sudden, my fingers touched something round and hard. When I pulled out my hand, I saw that it was a gold coin, on the front of which the Kraków Basilica was etched in all its glory.

'No way,' I whispered, showing it to Maya. She put her own hand in the pocket of her skirt and pulled out its twin.

'Just so we don't forget,' she said.

It went well. Quite a crowd arrived a good half-hour before the event was due to start and with ten minutes to go, there wasn't a single seat left. We saw a couple of our classmates standing at the back with their parents and did our best to squeeze as many people in as possible.

'What a turnout,' the professor said, addressing us all. 'I want to start by wholeheartedly thanking Konrad and Maya for inviting me to speak to you. As many of you will have heard, you live near a spot where a rather special discovery was made.'

He started by telling us about his work and where his interest in dinosaurs began. (Interestingly, it was through finding a much smaller fossil when he was young and living in Canada.) Then he spoke about the different species that he'd studied and showed us some great photos of the bones found at archaeological sites he'd worked on, and how they all fitted together.

'The trouble with dinosaurs is that there's always something missing. There are very, very few complete dinosaur skeletons out there in the world. Maybe that's the beauty of them? They leave a little bit of themselves to the imagination?'

Out of the corner of my eye, I spotted Luke. He'd been here with me and Dad a few times, and was glancing around curiously to see how things had changed. He caught my eye and gave me a half-smile.

'And as for the print that was discovered along your stretch of coastline,' said the professor. 'I don't know for certain what created this print. I can make several informed guesses. It is the right shape to belong to a Megalosaurus, but it isn't quite the right size.

'It's as if it was made by a slightly smaller animal. But I've noticed something peculiar about the tips of the claws. There's a visible speck in the rock just above the three prongs, which has led me to conclude that this animal had rounded claws, curling downwards. It could be that it hadn't had a manicure for a while, or perhaps we're dealing with a different animal entirely. That's what makes science so fascinating. There is always something more to discover…'

Maya and I looked at each other. I remembered the curled claw that I'd stroked outside the cave in a world so different to our own, but at the same time so very similar.

She squeezed my hand. We were the only ones who knew.

# A letter to you from Ewa

Dear Reader,

Do you love books, just like me? I've always thought of them as a gateway into so many brilliant different worlds. Imagine if you could step into one of them, not just in your imagination, but in real life? That's exactly what happens to Kon in *The Dragon in the Bookshop*.

The book features a Polish legend about the Wawel dragon of Kraków. He lived in a cave below the castle, had an insatiable appetite and terrorised the townspeople. No one knew how to get rid of him! As a child, I often wondered whether he was as bad as everyone made out. Perhaps the legend could be read in a different way? Maybe there was an important piece of context that we were missing?

*The Dragon in the Bookshop* is special to me, as the inspiration for it came from my dad who passed away when I was a teenager. He read me many stories and legends and truly ignited my love of reading. When he died, I missed him so much that I didn't really want to speak to anyone. Through the character of Kon, I've revisited those early emotions.

I also wanted to show that the people we lose, who are close to our hearts, are never really gone. They're in so many elements of what we do every day – in the things we say, the decisions we make, even the books we read.

I hope that apart from taking you on an exciting adventure, my story might offer reassurance to anyone who has been through a similar experience. On the next page you'll find some information about Grief Encounter, a wonderful charity working with young people who have lost someone important in their lives.

Happy reading –

*Ewa Jozefkowicz*

# gr·ef
# encounter

Grief Encounter is one of the UK's leading child bereavement charities providing professional support to children and young people following the death of a loved one.

Grief Encounter offers a wide range of bespoke, professional support, including counselling, workshops, retreats and family events, designed and developed by Dr Shelley Gilbert MBE. These are available for **free** and offer bereaved children and young people a safe space to grieve and talk about their feelings following the death of a parent or sibling.

Grieftalk is a confidential national helpline where trained counsellors provide instant support:

Call:    0808 802 0111 Weekdays 9am-9pm
Email: grieftalk@griefencounter.org.uk
Chat:  via the website

To find out more about what Grief Encounter does, and for ideas on how to fundraise or volunteer for this brilliant charity, check out:

**www.griefencounter.org.uk**

# Acknowledgements

Thank you to my publisher, Fiona Kennedy, for encouraging me to write *The Dragon in the Bookshop*. I realise now that the idea had been bubbling below the surface for many years and needed someone to coax it out. Thank you also to Lauren, Jade, Meg, Claire and the rest of the brilliant team at Zephyr.

Thank you to my wonderful agent Kate Hordern for your patience, encouragement and great plot advice.

Thank you to the very talented Katy Riddell who brought Kon, Maya and Yellow Eye so brilliantly to life on the cover.

Thank you to all my family and friends for helping me with my Polish legend research, and particularly to Deeps who went to Kraków with me in search of the dragon's lair.

Thank you to Giles for being a long-suffering sounding board, and for taking me to Dungeness on a trip all those years ago. I didn't realise at the time that I was looking at Kon's future house.

Thank you to Jean Gross for letting me borrow the beautiful idea of recorded books which help children remember a parent's voice (as written about in her daughter Kate's book *Late Fragments*).

Thank you to Lou, Sam and the incredible team at Grief Encounter for the really valuable work you do to support bereaved children and teenagers.

And perhaps most importantly, a belated thank you to my dad, without whom *The Dragon in the Bookshop*, or any of my other stories, probably wouldn't have been written. I miss you. I'm still searching for your character in a book, but I'm certain I'll find him.

Ewa Jozefkowicz
London 2022

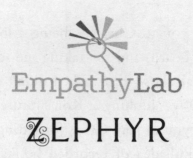

# EmpathyLab

## ZEPHYR

### We are an Empathy Builder Publisher

- Empathy is our ability to understand and share someone else's feelings
- It builds stronger, kinder communities
- It's a crucial life skill that can be learned

We are supporting **EmpathyLab** in their work to develop a book-based empathy movement in a drive to reach one million children a year and more.

Find out more at www.empathylab.uk
www.empathylab.uk/what-is-empathy-day

#EMPATHY DAY
Every June
empathylab.uk